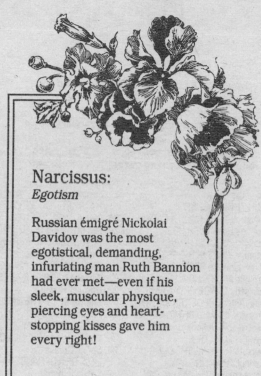

Narcissus:
Egotism

Russian émigré Nickolai Davidov was the most egotistical, demanding, infuriating man Ruth Bannion had ever met—even if his sleek, muscular physique, piercing eyes and heart-stopping kisses gave him every right!

NORA ROBERTS

LANGUAGE OF LOVE

**Love has a language all its own, and for
centuries, flowers have symbolized
love's finest expression.
Discover the language of flowers
—and love—
in this romantic collection of 48 favorite
books by bestselling author Nora Roberts.**

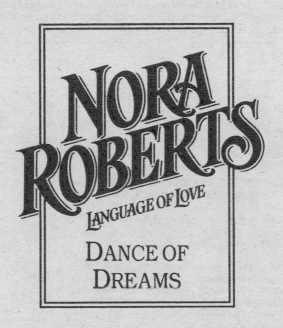

NORA ROBERTS

LANGUAGE OF LOVE

DANCE OF DREAMS

Silhouette Books®

SILHOUETTE BOOKS
300 East 42nd St., New York, N.Y. 10017

DANCE OF DREAMS © 1983 by Nora Roberts.
First published as a Silhouette Special Edition.

Language of Love edition published May 1992

ISBN: 0-373-51008-X

Printed in U.S.A.

Chapter One

The cat lay absolutely still on his back, eyes closed, front paws resting on his white chest. The last rays of the sun slanted through the long vertical blinds and shone on his orange fur. He was undisturbed by the sound of a key in the lock which broke the silence of the apartment. He half opened his eyes when he heard his mistress' voice but closed them again, just as lazily, when he noted she was not alone. She'd brought that man home with her again, and the cat had no liking for him. He went back to sleep.

"But Ruth, it's barely eight o'clock. The sun's still up."

Ruth dropped her keys on the dainty Queen Anne table beside the door, then turned with a smile. "Donald, I told you I had to make it an early evening. Dinner was lovely. I'm glad you talked me into going out."

"In that case," he said, taking her into his arms in a practiced move, "let me talk you into extending the evening."

Ruth accepted the kiss, enjoyed the gentle surge of warmth just under her skin. But when he pulled her closer, she drew away. "Donald." Her smile was the same easy one she had worn before the kiss. "You really have to go."

"A nightcap," he murmured, kissing her again, lightly, persuasively.

"Not tonight." She moved firmly out of his arms. "I have an early class tomorrow, Donald, plus a full day of rehearsals and fittings."

He gave her a quick kiss on the forehead. "It'd be easier for me if it were another man, but this passion for dancing...." He shrugged before reluctantly turning to leave. Was he losing his touch? he wondered.

Ruth Bannion was the first woman in over ten years who had held him off so consistently and successfully. Why, he asked himself, did he keep coming back? She opened the door for him, giving him one last, lingering smile as she urged him through. A glimpse of her silhouette in the dim light before she shut the door on him answered his question. She was more than beautiful—she was unique.

Ruth was still smiling as she hooked the chain and security lock. She enjoyed Donald Keyser. He was tall and dark and stylishly handsome, with an acerbic humor and exquisite taste. She respected his talents as a designer, wore a number of his creations herself and was able to relax in his company—when she found the time. Of course, she was aware that Donald would have preferred a more intimate relationship.

It had been a simple matter for Ruth to decide against it. She was attracted to Donald and was fond of him. But he simply did not stir her emotions. While she knew he could make her laugh, she doubted very much that he could make her cry. Turning into the darkened apartment, Ruth felt a twinge of regret. She felt abruptly, unexpectedly alone.

Ruth turned to study herself in the gilt-framed, rectangular mirror that hung in the hallway. It was one of the first pieces she had bought when she had moved into the apartment. The glass was old, and she had paid a ridiculous price for it, despite the dark spots near the top right-hand corner. It had meant a great deal to Ruth to be able to hang it on the wall of her own apartment, her own home. Now, as the light grew dim, she stared at her reflection.

She had left her hair down for this evening, and it flowed over her shoulders to swing past her elbows. With an impatient move, she tossed it back. It lifted, then settled behind her, black and thick. Her face, like her frame, was small and delicate, but her features weren't even. Her mouth was generous, her nose small and straight, her chin a subtle point. Though the bones in her face were elegant, the deep brown eyes were huge and slanted catlike. The brows over them were dark and straight. An exotic face, she had been told, yet she saw no beauty in it. She knew that with the right make-up and lighting she could look stunning, but that was different. That was an illusion, a role, not Ruth Bannion.

With a sigh, Ruth turned away from the mirror and crossed to the plush-covered Victorian sofa. Knowing she was now alone, Nijinsky rolled over, stretched and yawned luxuriously, then padded over to curl in her lap. Ruth scratched his ears absently. Who was Ruth Bannion? she wondered.

Five years before, she had been a very green, very eager student beginning a new phase of her training in New York. *Thanks to Lindsay,* Ruth remembered with a smile. Lindsay Dunne, teacher, friend, idol—the finest classical ballerina Ruth had ever seen. She had convinced Uncle Seth to let her come here. It warmed Ruth to think of them now, married, living in the Cliff House in Connecticut with their children. Every time she visited them, the love and happiness lingered with her for weeks afterward. She had never seen two people more right for each other or more in love. Except perhaps her own parents.

Even after six years, thinking of her parents brought on a wave of sadness—for herself and for the tragic loss of two bright, warm people. But in a strange way Ruth knew it had been their death that had brought her to where she was today.

Seth Bannion had become her guardian, and their move to the small seacoast town in Connecticut had brought them both to Lindsay. It had been through Lindsay that Seth had been made to see Ruth's need for more training. Ruth knew it hadn't been easy for her uncle to allow her to make the move to New York when she had been only seventeen. She had, of course, been well cared for by the Evanstons, but it had been difficult for Seth to give her up to a life he knew to be so difficult and demanding. It was love that had made him hesitate and love that had ultimately ruled his decision. Her life had changed forever.

Or perhaps, Ruth reflected, it had changed that first time she had walked into Lindsay's school to dance. It had been there that she had first danced for Davidov.

How terrified she had been! She had stood there in front of a man who had been heralded as the finest dancer of the decade. A master, a legend. Nikolai Davidov, who had partnered only the most gifted ballerinas, including Lindsay Dunne. Indeed, he had come to Connecticut to convince Lindsay to return to New York as the star in a ballet he had written. Ruth had been overwhelmed by his presence and almost too stunned to move when he had ordered her to dance for him. But he had been charming. A smile touched Ruth's mouth as she leaned her head back on the cushions. And who, she thought lazily, could be more charming than Nick when he chose to be? She had obeyed, losing herself in the movement and the music. Then he had spoken those simple, stunning words.

"When you come to New York, come to me."

She had been very young and had thought of Nikolai Davidov as a name to be whispered reverently. She would have danced barefoot down Broadway if he had told her to.

She had worked hard to please him, terrified of the sting of his temper, unable to bear the coldness of his disapproval. And he had pushed her. Ruth remembered how he had been constantly, mercilessly demanding. There had been nights she had curled up in bed, too exhausted to even weep. But then he would smile or toss off a compliment, and every moment of pain would vanish.

She had danced with him, fought with him, laughed with him, watched the gradual changes in him over the years, and still, there was an elusive quality about him.

Perhaps that was the secret of his attraction for women, she thought: the subtle air of mystery, his foreign accent, his reticence about his past. She had gotten over her infatuation with him years ago. She smiled, remembering the intensity of her crush on him. He hadn't appeared to even notice it. She had been scarcely eighteen. He'd been nearly thirty and surrounded by beautiful women. And *still is,* she reminded herself, smiling in rueful amusement as she stood up to stretch. The cat, now dislodged from her lap, stalked huffily away.

My heart's whole and safe, Ruth decided. Perhaps too safe. She thought of Donald. Well, it couldn't be helped. She yawned and stretched again. And there was that early class in the morning.

Sweat dampened Ruth's T-shirt. Nick's choreography for *The Red Rose* was complicated and strenuous. She took a much-needed breather at the barre. The remainder of the cast was scattered around the rehearsal hall, either dancing under Nick's unflagging instructions or waiting, as she did, for the next summons.

It was only eleven, but Ruth had already worked through a two-hour morning class. The long, loose T-shirt she wore over her tights was darkened by patches of perspiration; a few tendrils of her hair had escaped from her tightly secured bun. Still, watching Nick demonstrate a move, any thought of fatigue drained from her. He was, she thought as she always did, absolutely fabulous.

As artistic director of the company and as established creator of ballets, he no longer had to dance to remain in the limelight. He danced, Ruth knew, because he was born to do so. He skimmed just under six feet, but his lean, wiry build gave an illusion of more height. His hair was like gold dust and curled carelessly around a face that had never completely lost its boyish charm. His mouth was beautiful, full and finely sculpted. And when he smiled...

When he smiled, there was no resisting him. Fine lines would spread out from his eyes, and the large irises would become incredibly blue.

Watching him demonstrate a turn, Ruth was grateful that at thirty-three, with all his other professional obligations, he still continued to dance.

He stopped the pianist with a flick of his hand. "All right, children," he said in his musically Russian-accented voice. "It could be worse."

This from Davidov, Ruth mused wryly, was close to an accolade.

"Ruth, the *pas de deux* from the first act."

She crossed to him instantly, giving an absent brush at the locks of hair that danced around her face. Nick was a creature of moods—varied, mercurial, unexplained moods. Today he appeared to be all business. Ruth knew how to match his temperament with her own. Facing, they touched right hands, palm to palm. Without a word, they began.

It was an early love scene, more a duel of wits than an expression of romance. But Nick hadn't written a fairy tale ballet this time. He had written a passionate one. The characters were a prince and a gypsy, each fiercely flesh and blood. To accommodate them, the dances were exuberant and athletic. They challenged each other; he demanded, she defied. Now and then a toss of the head or a gesture of the wrist was employed to accent the mood.

The late summer sun poured through the windows, patterning the floor. Drops of sweat trickled unheeded, unfelt, down Ruth's back as she turned in, then out of Nick's arms. The character of Carlotta would enrage and enrapture the prince throughout the ballet. The mood for their duel of hearts was set during their first encounter.

It was at times like this, when Ruth danced with Nick, that she realized she would always worship him, the dancer, the legend. To be his partner was the greatest thrill of her life. He took her beyond herself, beyond what she had ever hoped to be. On her journey from student to the *corps de ballet* to principal dancer, Ruth had danced with many partners, but none of them could touch Nick Davidov for sheer brilliance and precision. And endurance, she thought ruefully as he ordered the *pas de deux* to begin again.

Ruth took a moment to catch her breath as the pianist turned back the pages of the score. Nick turned to her, lifting his hand for hers. "Where is your passion today, little one?" he demanded.

It was a salutation Ruth detested, and he knew it. The grin shot across his face as she glared at him. Saying nothing, she placed her palm to his.

"Now, my gypsy, tell me to go to the devil with your body as well as your eyes. Again."

They began, but this time Ruth stopped thinking of her pleasure in dancing with him. She competed now, step for step, leap for leap. Her annoyance gave Nick precisely what he wanted. She dared him to best her. She spun into his arms, her eyes hot. Poised only a moment, she spun away again and with a *grand jeté,* challenged him to follow her.

They ended as they had begun, palm to palm, with her head thrown back. Laughing, Nick caught her close and kissed her enthusiastically on both cheeks.

"There, now, you're wonderful! You spit at me even while you offer your hand."

Ruth's breath was coming quickly after the effort of the dance. Her eyes, still lit with temper, remained on Nick's. A swift flutter raced up her spine, distracting her. She saw that Nick had felt it, too. She saw it in his eyes, felt it in the fingers he pressed into the small of her back. Then it was gone, and Nick drew her away.

"Lunch," he stated and earned a chorus of approval. The rehearsal hall began to clear immediately. "Ruth." Nick took her hand as she turned to join the others. "I want to talk to you."

"All right, after lunch."

"Now. Here."

Her brows drew together. "Nick, I missed breakfast—"

"There's yogurt in the refrigerator downstairs, and Perrier." Releasing her hand, Nick walked to the piano. He sat and began to improvise. "Bring some for me, too."

Hands on her hips, Ruth watched him play. Of course, she thought wrathfully, he'd never consider I'd say no. He'd never think to ask me if I had other plans. He expects I'll run off like a good little girl and do his bidding without a word of complaint.

"Insufferable," she said aloud.

Nick glanced up but continued to play. "Did you speak?" he asked mildly.

"Yes," she answered distinctly. "I said, you're insufferable."

"Yes." Nick smiled at her good-humoredly. "I am."

Despite herself, Ruth laughed. "What flavor?" she demanded and was pleased when he gave her a blank look. "Yogurt," she reminded him. "What flavor yogurt, Davidov."

In short order Ruth's arms were ladened with cartons of yogurt, spoons, glasses and a large bottle of Perrier. There was the sound of chatter from the canteen below her mingling with Nick's playing the piano from the hall above. She climbed the stairs, exchanging remarks with two members of the *corps* and a male soloist. The music Nick played was a low, bluesy number. Because she recognized the style, Ruth knew it to be one of his own compositions. No, not a composition, she corrected as she paused in the door-way to watch him. A composition you write down, preserve. This is music that comes from the heart.

The sun's rays fell over his hair and his hands—long, narrow hands with fluid fingers that could express more with a gesture than the average person could with a speech.

He looks so alone!

The thought sped into her mind unexpectedly, catching her off balance. It's the music, she decided. It's only because he plays such sad music. She walked toward him, her ballet shoes making no sound on the wood floor.

"You look lonely, Nick."

From the way his head jerked up, Ruth knew she had broken into some deep, private thought. He looked at her oddly a moment, his fingers poised above the piano keys. "I was," he said. "But that's not what I want to talk to you about."

Ruth arched a brow. "Is this going to be a business lunch?" she asked him as she set cartons of yogurt on the piano.

"No." He took the bottle of Perrier, turning the cap. "Then we'd argue, and that's bad for the digestion, yes? Come, sit beside me."

Ruth sat on the bench, automatically steeling herself for the jolt of electricity. To be where he was was to be in the vortex of power. Even now, relaxed, contemplating a simple dancer's lunch, he was like a circuit left on hold.

"Is there a problem?" she asked, reaching for a carton of yogurt and a spoon.

"That's what I want to know."

Puzzled, she turned her head to find him studying her face. He had bottomless blue eyes, clear as glass, and the dancer's ability for complete stillness.

"What do you mean?"

"I had a call from Lindsay." The blue eyes were fixed unwaveringly on hers. His lashes were the color of the darkest shade of his hair.

More confused, Ruth wrinkled her brow. "Oh?"

"She thinks you're not happy." He was still watching her steadily; the pressure began to build at the base of her neck. Ruth turned away, and it lessened immediately. There had never been anyone else who could unnerve her with a look.

"Lindsay worries too much," she said lightly, dipping the spoon into the yogurt.

"Are you, Ruth?" Nick laid his hand on her arm, and she was compelled to look back at him. "Are you unhappy?"

"No," she said immediately, truthfully. She gave him the slow half smile that was so much a part of her. "No."

He continued to scan her face as his hand slid down to her wrist. "Are you happy?"

She opened her mouth, prepared to answer, then closed it again on a quick sound of frustration. Why must those eyes be on hers, so direct, demanding perfect honesty? They wouldn't accept platitudes or pat answers. "Shouldn't I be?" she countered. His fingers tightened on her wrist as she started to rise.

"Ruth." She had no choice but to face him again. "Are we friends?"

She fumbled for an answer. A simple yes hardly covered the complexities of her feelings for him or the uneven range of their relationship. "Sometimes," she answered cautiously. "Sometimes we are."

Nick accepted that, though amusement lit his eyes. "Well said," he murmured. Unexpectedly, he gathered both of her hands in his and brought them to his lips. His mouth was soft as a whisper on her skin. Ruth didn't pull away but stiffened, surprised and wary. His eyes met hers placidly over their joined hands, as if he were unaware of her would-be withdrawal. "Will you tell me why you're not happy?"

Carefully, coolly, Ruth drew her hands from him. It was too difficult to behave in a contained manner when touching him. He was a physical man, demanding physical response. Rising, Ruth walked across the room to a window. Manhattan hustled by below.

"To be perfectly honest," she began thoughtfully, "I haven't given my happiness much thought. Oh, no," she laughed and shook her head. "That sounds pompous." She spun back to face him, but he wasn't smiling. "Nick, I only meant that until you asked me, I just hadn't thought about being unhappy." She shrugged and leaned back against the window sill. Nick poured some fizzling water and rising, took it to her.

"Lindsay's worried about you."

"Lindsay has enough to worry about with Uncle Seth and the children and her school."

"She loves you," he said simply.

He saw it—the slow smile, the darkening warmth in her eyes, the faintly mystified pleasure. "Yes, I know she does."

"That surprises you?" Absently, he wound a loose tendril of her hair around his finger. It was soft and slightly damp.

"Her generosity astonishes me. I suppose it always will." She paused a moment, then continued quickly before she lost her nerve. "Were you ever in love with her?"

"Yes," he answered instantly, without embarrassment or regret. "Years ago, briefly." He smiled and pushed one of Ruth's loosened pins back into her hair. "She was always just out of my reach. Then before I knew it, we were friends."

"Strange," she said after a moment. "I can't imagine you considering anything out of your reach."

Nick smiled again. "I was very young, the age you are now. And it's you we're speaking of, Ruth, not Lindsay. She thinks perhaps I push you too hard."

"Push too hard?" Ruth cast her eyes at the ceiling. "*You*, Nikolai?"

He gave her his haughtily amused look. "I, too, was astonished."

Ruth shook her head, then moved back to the piano. She exchanged Perrier for yogurt. "I'm fine, Nick. I hope you told her so." When he didn't answer, Ruth turned, the spoon still between her lips. "Nick?"

"I thought perhaps you've had an unhappy...relationship."

Her brows lifted. "Do you mean, Am I unhappy over a lover?"

It was instantly apparent that he hadn't cared for her choice of words. "You're very blunt, little one."

"I'm not a child," she countered testily, then slapped the carton onto the piano again. "And I don't—"

"Do you still see the designer?" Nick interrupted her coolly.

"The designer has a name," she said sharply. "Donald Keyser. You make him sound like a label on a dress."

"Do I?" Nick gave her a guileless smile. "But you don't answer my question."

"No, I don't." Ruth lifted the glass of Perrier and sipped calmly, though a flash of temper leaped into her eyes.

"Ruth, are you still seeing him?"

"That's none of your business." She made her voice light, but the steel was beneath it.

"You are a member of the company." Though his eyes blazed into hers, he enunciated each word carefully. "I am the director."

"Have you also taken over the role of Father Confessor?" Ruth tossed back. "Must your dancers check out their lovers with you?"

"Be careful how you provoke me," he warned.

"I don't have to justify my social life to you, Nick," she shot back without a pause. "I go to class, I'm on time for rehearsals. I work hard."

"Did I ask you to justify anything?"

"Not really. But I'm tired of you playing the role of stern uncle with me." A frown line ran down between her brows as she stepped closer to him. "I have an uncle already, and I don't need you to look over my shoulder."

"Don't you?" He plucked a loose pin from her hair and twirled it idly between his thumb and forefinger while his eyes pierced into hers.

His casual tone fanned her fury. "No!" She tossed her head. "Stop treating me like a child."

Nick gripped her shoulders, surprising her with the quick violence. She was drawn hard against him, molded to the body she knew so well. But this was different. There were no music or steps or storyline. She could feel his anger—and something more, something just as volatile. She knew he was capable of sudden bursts of rage, and she knew how to deal with them, but now...

Her body was responding, astonishing her. Their hearts beat against each other. She could feel his fingertips digging into her flesh, but there was no pain. The hands she had brought up to shove him away with were now balled into fists and held motionlessly aloft.

He dropped his eyes to her lips. A sharp pang of longing struck her—sharper, sweeter than anything she had ever experienced. It left her dazed and aching.

Slowly, knowing only that what she wanted was a breath away, Ruth leaned forward, letting her lids sink down in preparation for his kiss. His breath whispered on her lips, and hers parted. She said his name once, wonderingly.

Then, with a jerk and a muttered Russian oath, Nikolai pushed her away. "You should know better," he said, biting off the words, "than to deliberately make me angry."

"Was that what you were feeling?" she asked, stung by his rejection.

"Don't push it." Nick tossed off the American slang with a movement of his shoulders. Temper lingered in his eyes. "Stick with your designer," he murmured at length in a quieter tone as he turned back to the piano. "Since he seems to suit you so well."

He sat again and began to play, dismissing her with silence.

Chapter Two

She must have imagined it. Ruth relived the surge of concentrated desire she had experienced in Nick's arms. No, I'm wrong, she told herself again. I've been in his arms countless times and never, never felt anything like that. And, Ruth reminded herself as she showered off the grime of the day, I was in his arms a half-dozen times after, when we went back to rehearsal.

There had been something, she admitted grudgingly as she recalled the crackling tension in the air when they had gone over a passage time and time again. But it had been annoyance, aggravation.

Ruth let the water flow and stream over her, plastering her hair to her naked back. She tried, now that she was alone, to figure out her reaction to Nick's sudden embrace.

Her response had been nakedly physical and shockingly urgent. On the other hand, she could recall the warm pleasure of Donald's kisses—the soft, easily resisted temptation. Donald used quiet words and gentle persuasion. He used all the traditional trappings of seduction: flowers, candlelight, intimate dinners. He made her feel—Ruth grasped for a word. *Pleasant.* She rolled her eyes, knowing no man would be flattered with that description. Yet she had never experienced more than *pleasant* with Donald or any other man she had known. And then, in one brief moment, a man she had worked with for years, a man who could infuriate her with a word or move her to tears with a dance, had caused an eruption inside her. There had been nothing *pleasant* about it.

He never kissed me, she mused, losing herself for a moment in the remembering. Or even held me, really—not as a lover would, but . . .

It was an accident, she told herself and switched off the shower with a jerk of her wrist. A fluke. Just a chain reaction from the passion of the dance and the anger of the argument.

Standing naked and wet, Ruth reached for a towel to dry herself. She began with her hair. Her body was small and delicately built, thin by all but a dancer's standards. She knew it intimately, as only a dancer could. Her limbs were long and slender and supple. It had been her classical dancer's build—and the fateful events of her life—that had brought her to Lindsay years before.

Lindsay, Ruth smiled, remembering vividly her fiery dancing in *Don Quixote,* a ballet Lindsay had starred in before she and Ruth had met. Ruth's smile became wry as she recalled her first face-to-face meeting with the older dancer. It had been years later, in Lindsay's small ballet school. Ruth had been both awed and terrified. She had stated boldly that one day she, too, would dance in *Don Quixote!*

And she had, Ruth remembered, wrapping a towel around her slim body. And Uncle Seth and Lindsay had come, even though Lindsay had been nearly eight months pregnant at the time. Lindsay had cried, and Nick had joked and teased her.

With a sigh, Ruth dropped the towel in a careless heap and reached for her robe. Only Lindsay would have guessed that all was not quite right. Ruth belted the thin fuchsia robe and picked up a comb. She had spoken of Donald, she remembered, playing back their last phone conversation. She had told them about the fabulous little chest she had found in the Village. They had chatted about the children, and Uncle Seth had begged her to come visit them her first free weekend.

And through all the tidbits and family gossip, Lindsay sensed something she hadn't even realized herself. Ruth frowned. That she wasn't happy. Not unhappy, she thought and took the comb smoothly through her long, wet hair. Just dissatisfied. Silly, she decided, annoyed with herself. She had everything she'd ever wanted. She was a principal dancer with the company, a recognized name in the world of ballet. She would be starring in Davidov's latest ballet. The work was hard and demanding, but Ruth craved it. It was the life she had been born for.

But still, sometimes, she longed to break the rules, to race back to the vagabond time she had known as a child. There had been such freedom, such adventure. Her eyes lit with the memories: skiing in Switzerland where the air was so cold and clean it had hurt her throat to breathe it; the smells and colors of Istanbul. The thin, large-eyed children in the streets of Crete; a funny little room with glass doorknobs in Bonn. All those years she had traveled with her journalist parents. Had they ever been more than three months in one place? It had been impossible to form any strong attachments, except to each other. And to the dance. That had been her constant childhood companion, traveling with her in an ever-changing environment. The teachers had spoken with different voices, different accents, in different languages, but the dance had remained there for her.

The years of travel had given Ruth an early maturity; there was no shyness, only self-sufficiency and caution. Then came her life with Seth, then Lindsay, and her years with the Evanston family that had opened her up, encouraging her to offer trust and affection. Still her world remained insular, as only the world of ballet can be. Perhaps because of this she was an inveterate observer. Watching and analyzing people was more than a habit with Ruth; it had become her nature.

And it was this that had led to her further annoyance with Nick. She had watched him that afternoon and sensed disturbances, but she hadn't been able to put a name to them. What he had been thinking and feeling remained a mystery. Ruth didn't care for mysteries.

That's why Donald appeals to me, she mused with a half-smile. She toyed with the bottles of powder and scent on her dressing table. He's so unpretentious, so predictable. His thoughts and feelings are right on the surface. No eddies, no undercurrents. But with a man like Nick...

She poured lotion into her palm and worked it over her arms. A man like Nick, she thought, was totally unpredictable, a constant source of annoyance and confusion. Volatile, unreasonable, exhausting. Just trying to keep up with him wore her out. And it was so difficult to please him! She had seen many dancers push themselves beyond endurance to give him what he wanted. She did it herself. What was it about him that was endlessly fascinating?

A knock on her door broke into Ruth's thoughts. She shrugged, turning away from the dressing table. It was no use trying to dissect Nikolai Davidov. She flipped on a light in the living room as she rushed through it to the front door. Her glance through the peephole surprised her. She drew the chain from the door.

"Donald, I was just thinking about you."

She was swept up in his arms before she had the chance to offer him a friendly kiss. *"Mmm,* you smell wonderful."

Her laugh was smothered by his lips. The kiss grew long, deeper than the casual greeting Ruth had intended. Yet she allowed the intimacy, encouraging it with her own seeking tongue. She wanted to feel, to experience more than the warm pleasure she was accustomed to. She wanted the excitement, the tingling touch of fear she had felt only that afternoon in another man's arms. But when it was over, her heart-beat was steady, her blood cool.

"Now that," Donald murmured and nuzzled her neck, "is the way to say hello."

Ruth stayed in his arms a moment, enjoying his solidarity, the unspoken offer of protection. Then, pulling away, she smiled into his eyes. "It's also a way of saying it's nice to see you, but what are you doing here?"

"Taking you out," he said and swung her further into the room. "Go put on your prettiest dress," he ordered, giving her cheek a brief caress. "One of mine, of course. We're going to a party."

Ruth pushed her still-damp hair away from her face. "A party?"

"Hmm—yes." Donald glanced at Nijinsky, who lay sprawled in sleep on Ruth's small glass-topped dinette table. "A party at Germaine Jones's," he continued as he and the cat ignored each other. "You remember, the designer who's pushing her short, patterned skirts and knee socks."

"Yes, I remember." **Ruth** had the quick impression of a short, pixielike redhead with sharp green eyes and thick, mink lashes. "I wish you'd called first."

"I did—or tried to," he put in. "It's a spur-of-the-moment thing, but I did phone the rehearsal hall. I missed you there, and you hadn't gotten home yet." He shrugged away the oversight as he drew out his slim, gold cigarette case. "Germaine's throwing the party together at the last minute, but a lot of important people will show. She's hot this season." Donald slipped the case back into the inside pocket of his smartly tailored slate-colored suit jacket, then flicked on his lighter.

"I can't make it tonight."

Lifting a brow, Donald blew out a stream of smoke. "Why not?" He took in her wet hair and thin robe. "You don't have plans, do you?"

Ruth was tempted to contradict him. He was beginning to take too much for granted. "Is that such a remote possibility, Donald?" she asked, masking her annoyance with a smile.

"Of course not." He grinned disarmingly. "But somehow I don't think you do. Now be a good girl and slip into that red slinky number. Germaine's bound to have on one of her famous ensembles. You'll make her look like a misplaced cheerleader."

She studied him a moment, with her dark eyes thoughtful. "You're not always kind, are you, Donald?"

"It's not a kind business, darling." He shrugged an elegant shoulder.

Ruth bit back a sigh. She knew he was fond of her and undeniably attracted, but she wondered if he would be quite so fond or so attracted if he didn't consider her to be an asset when she wore one of his designs. "I'm sorry, Donald, I'm just not up to a party tonight."

"Oh, come on, Ruth." He tapped his cigarette in the ashtray, his first sign of impatience. "All you have to do is look beautiful and speak to a few of the right people."

Ruth banked down on a rising surge of irritation. She knew Donald had never understood the demands and rigors of her profession.

"Donald," she began patiently. "I've been working since eight this morning. I'm bone tired. If I don't get the proper rest, I won't be able to function at top level tomorrow. I have a responsibility to the rest of the company, to Nick and to myself."

Carefully, Donald stubbed out the cigarette. Smoke hung in the air for a moment, then wafted out through an open window. "You can't tell me you won't do any socializing, Ruth. That's absurd."

"Not as absurd as you think," she returned, crossing to him. "There're less than three weeks until the ballet opens, Donald. Parties simply have to wait until after."

"And me, Ruth?" He pulled her into his arms. Underneath his calm, civilized exterior, she sensed the anger. "How long do I have to wait?"

"I've never promised you anything, Donald. You've known from the beginning that my work is my first priority. Just as your work is for you."

"Does that mean you have to keep denying that you're a woman?"

Ruth's eyes remained calm, but her tone chilled. "I don't believe I've done that."

"Don't you?" Donald's hold on her tightened, just as Nick's had hours before. She found it interesting that the two men should draw two such differing responses from her. With Nick she had felt equal anger and a sharp attraction. Now she felt only impatience touched with fatigue.

"Donald, I'm hardly denying my womanhood by not going to bed with you."

"You know how much I want you." He pulled her closer. "Every time I touch you, I feel you give up to a certain point. Then it stops, just as if you've thrown up a wall." His voice roughened with frustration. "How long are you going to lock me out?"

Ruth felt a pang of guilt. She knew he spoke the truth, just as she knew there was nothing she could do to alter it. "I'm sorry, Donald."

He read the regret in her eyes and changed tactics. Drawing her close again, he spoke softly, his eyes warming. "You know how I feel about you, darling." His lips took hers quietly, persuasively. "We could leave the party early, bring a bottle of champagne back here."

"Donald. You don't—" she began. Another knock at the door interrupted her. Distracted, she didn't bother with the peephole before sliding the chain. "Nick!" She stared at him foolishly, her mind wiped clean.

"Do you open the door to everyone?" he asked in mild censure as he entered without invitation. "Your hair's wet," he added, taking a generous handful. "And you smell like the first rain in spring."

It was as if the angry words had never been spoken, as if the simmering, restrained passion had never been. He was smiling down at her, an amused cocky look in his eyes. Bending, he kissed her nose.

Ruth made a face as she pulled her thoughts into order. "I wasn't expecting you."

"I was passing," he said, "and saw your lights."

At the sound of Nick's voice, Nijinsky leaped from the table to rub affectionate circles around the dancer's ankles. Stooping, Nick stroked him once from neck to tail and laughed when the cat rose on his hind legs to jump at him affectionately. Nick rose, with Nijinsky purring audibly in his arms, then spotted Donald across the room.

"Hello." There was no apparent change in his amiability.

"You remember Donald," Ruth began hurriedly, guilty that for a moment she had completely forgotten him.

"Naturally." Nick continued to lazily scratch Nijinsky's ears. Purring ferociously, the cat stared with glinted amber eyes at the other man. "I saw a dress of your design on a mutual friend, Suzanne Boyer." Nick smiled with a flash of white teeth. "They were both exquisite."

Donald lifted a brow. "Thank you."

"But you don't offer me a drink, Ruth?" Nick commented, still smiling affably at Donald.

"Sorry," she murmured, automatically turning toward the small bar she had arranged on a drop leaf table in a corner. She reached for the vodka and poured. "Donald?"

"Scotch," he said briefly, trying to maintain some distance from Nick's cheerful friendliness.

Ruth handed Donald his Scotch and walked to Nick.

"Thanks." Accepting the glass, Nick sat in an overstuffed armchair and allowed the cat to walk tight circles on his lap. Nijinsky settled back to sleep while Nick drank. "Your business goes well?" he asked Donald.

"Yes, well enough," Donald responded to Nick's inquiry. He remained standing and sipped his Scotch.

"You use many plaids in your fall designs." Nick drank the undiluted vodka with a true Russian disregard for its potency.

"That's right." A hint of curiosity intruded into Donald's carefully neutral voice. "I didn't imagine you'd follow women's fashions."

"I follow women," Nick countered and drank again deeply. "I enjoy them."

It was a flat statement meant to be taken at face value. There were no sexual overtones. Nick enjoyed many women, Ruth knew, on many levels—from warm, pure friendships, as his relationship with Lindsay, to hot, smoldering affairs like that with their mutual friend Suzanne Boyer. His romances were the constant speculation of the tabloids.

"I think," Nick continued, disrupting Ruth's thoughts, "that you, too, enjoy women—and what makes them beautiful, interesting. It shows in your designs."

"I'm flattered." Donald relaxed enough to take a seat on the sofa.

"I never flatter," Nick returned with a quick, crooked smile. "A waste of words. Ruth will tell you I'm a very frugal man."

"Frugal?" Ruth lifted a brow, pursing her lips as if tasting the word. "No, I think the word is egocentric."

"The child had great respect once upon a time," Nick said into his empty glass.

"When I was a child, yes," she retorted. "I know you better now."

Something flashed in his eyes as he looked at her; anger, challenge, amusement—perhaps all three. She wasn't certain. She kept her eyes level.

"Do you?" he murmured, then set the glass aside. "You would think she'd have more awe for men of our age," he said mildly to Donald.

"Donald doesn't demand awe," she returned, hardly realizing how quickly she was becoming heated. "And he doesn't care for me to think of him as aged and wise."

"Fortunate," Nick decided as neither of them so much as glanced at the man they were discussing. "Then he won't have to adjust his expectations." He gently stroked Nijinsky's back. "She has a nasty tongue as well."

"Only for a select few," Ruth responded.

Nick tilted his head, shooting his disarmingly charming smile. "It's my turn to be flattered, it seems."

Blast him! she thought furiously. Never at a loss for an answer.

Regally, Ruth rose. Her body moved fluidly under the silk of her robe. Donald's gaze flicked down a moment, but Nick's remained on her face. "Like you," she said to him with a cool smile, "I find flattery a waste of time and words. You'll have to excuse me," she continued. "Donald and I are going to a party. I have to change."

There was some satisfaction to be gained from turning her back on him and walking away. She closed her bedroom door firmly. Impatiently, she grabbed the red dress out of her closet, pulled lingerie from her drawers and flung the heap onto the bed. Stripping out of the robe, she started to toss it aside when she heard the doorknob turn. Instinctively she held the robe in front of her, clutching it with both hands at her breasts. Her eyes were wide and astonished as Nick stalked into the room. He shut the door behind him.

"You can't come in here," she began on a rush, too surprised to be outraged or embarrassed.

Ignoring her, Nick crossed the room. "I am in here."

"Well, you can just turn around and get out." Ruth shifted the robe higher, realizing impotently that she was at a dread disadvantage. "I'm not dressed," she pointed out needlessly.

Nick's eyes flickered briefly and without apparent interest over her naked shoulders. "You appear adequately covered." The eyes shot back to her face and locked on hers. "Isn't a twelve-hour day enough for you, Ruth? You have an eight o'clock class in the morning."

"I know what time my class is," she retorted. Cautiously, she took one hand from the robe to push back her hair. "I don't need you to remind me of my schedule, Nick, any more than I need your approval of what I do with my free time."

"You do when it interferes with your performance for me."

She frowned as he stepped onto artistic ground. "You've had no reason to complain about my performance."

"Not yet," he agreed. "But I want your best—and you can hardly give me that if you exhaust yourself with these silly parties—"

"I have always given you my best, Nick," she tossed back. "But since when has every ounce of effort and sweat been enough for you?" She started to swirl away from him, remembered the robe no longer covered her flank and simmered in frustrated rage. "Would you please go?"

"I take what I need," he shot back, again overlooking her heated request. "Not so many years ago, *milaya,* you were eager to give it to me."

"That's not fair!" The jibe stung. "I still am. When I am working, there's nothing I won't give to you. But my private life is just that—private. Stop playing daddy, Nick. I've grown up."

"Is that all you want?" His burst of fury stunned her, so that she took an automatic step back. "Is being treated as a woman what is important to you?"

"I'm sick of you treating me as if I were still seventeen and ready to bend at the knee when you walk into a room." Her anger grew to match his. "I'm a responsible adult, able to look after myself."

"A responsible adult." His eyes narrowed, and Ruth recognized the danger signals. "Shall I show you how I treat responsible adults who also happen to be women?"

"No!"

But she was already in his arms, already molded close. It wasn't the hard, overpowering kiss she might have expected and fought against. He kissed as if he knew she would respond to him with equal fervor. It was a man's mouth seeking a woman's. There was no need for persuasion or force.

Ruth's lips parted when his did. Their tongues met. Her thoughts, her body, her world concentrated fully and completely on him. The scent of her bath rose between them. Reaching up to draw him closer, Ruth took her hands from the robe. It dropped unheeded to the floor. Nick ran his hands down her naked back, much as he had done to the cat, one long, smooth stroke. With a low sound of pleasure, Ruth pressed closer.

And as he ran his hands up her sides to linger there, the kiss grew deeper, beyond what she knew and into the uncharted.

Her head fell back in submission as she tangled her fingers in his hair. She pulled him closer, demanding that he take all she offered. It was a dark, pungent world she had never tasted, and she yearned. Her body quivered with hot need as his hands ran over her. She had felt them on her countless times in the past, steadying her, lifting her, coaching her. But there was no music to bring them together here, no planned choreography, only instinct and desire.

When she felt herself being drawn away from him, Ruth protested, straining closer. But his hands came firmly to her shoulders, and they were separated.

Ruth stood naked before him, making no attempt to cover herself. She knew he had already seen her soul; there was no need to conceal her body. Nick took his eyes down her, slowly, carefully, as if he would memorize every inch. Then his eyes were back on hers, darkened, penetrating. There was fury in them. Without a word, he turned and left the room.

Ruth heard the front door slam, and she knew he had gone.

Chapter Three

And one, and two, and three, and four. Ruth made the moves to the time Nick called. After hours of dancing, her body was beyond pain. She was numb. The scant four hours sleep had not given her time to recharge. It had been her own anger and a need to defy which had kept her at the noisy, smoke-choked party until the early hours of the morning. She knew that, just as she knew her dancing was well below par that day.

There was no scathing comment from Nick, no bout of temper. He simply called out the combinations again and again. He didn't shout when she missed her timing or swear when her pirouettes were shaky. When he partnered her, there were no teases, no taunts in her ear.

It would be easier, Ruth thought as she stretched to a slow *arabesque,* if he'd shouted or scolded her for doing what he had warned her against. But Nick had simply lowered her into a fish dive without saying a word.

If he had shouted, she could have shouted back and released some of her self-disgust. But he gave her no excuse through the classes and hours of rehearsals to lose her temper. Each time their eyes met, he seemed to look through her. She was only a body, an object moving to his music.

When Nick called a break, Ruth went to the back of the room and, sitting on the floor, brought her knees to her chest and rested her forehead on them. Her feet were cramping, but she lacked the energy to massage them. When someone draped a towel around her neck, she glanced up.

"Francie." Ruth managed a grateful smile.

"You look bushed."

"I am," Ruth returned. She used the towel to wipe perspiration from her face.

Francie Myers was a soloist, a talented, dedicated dancer and one of the first friends Ruth had made in the company. She was small and lean with soft, fawn-colored hair and sharp, black eyes. She was constantly acquiring and losing lovers with perpetual cheerfulness. Ruth admired her unabashed honesty and optimism.

"Are you sick?" Francie asked, slipping a piece of gum into her mouth.

Ruth rested her head against the wall. Someone was idling at the piano. The room was abuzz with conversation and music. "I was at a miserably crowded party until three o'clock in the morning."

"Sounds like fun." Francie stretched her leg up to touch the wall behind her, then back. She glanced at Ruth's shadowed eyes. "But I don't think your timing was too terrific."

Ruth shook her head with a sigh. "And I didn't even want to be there."

"Then what were you doing there?"

"Being perverse," Ruth muttered, shooting a quick glance at Nick.

"That takes the fun out of it." Francie's eyes darted across the room and landed on an elegant blond in a pale blue leotard. "Leah's had a few comments about your style today."

Ruth followed Francie's gaze. Leah's golden hair was pulled back from a beautifully sculptured ivory-skinned face. She was talking to Nick now, gesturing with her long, graceful hands.

"I'm sure she did."

"You know how badly she wanted the lead in this ballet," Francie went on. "Even dancing Aurora hasn't pacified her. Nick isn't dancing in *Sleeping Beauty*."

"Competition keeps the company alive," Ruth said absently, watching Nick smile and shake his head at Leah.

"And jealousy," Francie added.

Ruth turned her head again, meeting the dark, sharp eyes. "Yes," she agreed after a moment. "And jealousy."

The piano switched to a romantic ballad, and someone began to sing.

"Nothing's wrong with a little jealousy." Francie rhythmically circled her ankles one at a time. "It's healthy. But Leah..." Her small, piquant face was abruptly serious. "She's poison. If she wasn't such a beautiful dancer, I'd wish her in another company. Watch her," she added as she rose. "She'll do anything to get what she wants. She wants to be the prima ballerina of this company, and you're in her way.''

Thoughtfully, Ruth stood as Francie moved away. The attractive dancer rarely spoke ill of anyone. Perhaps she was overreacting to something Leah had said. Ruth had felt Leah's jealousy. There was always jealousy in the company, as there was in any family. It was a fact of life. Ruth also knew how badly Leah had wanted the part of Carlotta in Nick's new ballet.

They had competed for a great number of roles since their days in the *corps*. Each had won, and each had lost. Their styles were diverse, so that the roles each created were uniquely individual. Ruth was an athletic, passionate dancer. Leah was an elegant dancer—classic, refined, cool. She had a polished grace that Ruth admired but never tried to emulate. Her dancing was from the heart; Leah's was from the head. In technical skills they were as equal as two dancers could be. Ruth danced in *Don Quixote,* while Leah performed in *Giselle.* Ruth was the Firebird, while Leah was Princess Aurora. Nick used them both to the best advantage. And Ruth would be his Carlotta.

Now, watching her across the room, Ruth wondered if the jealousy was more deeply centered than she had sensed. Though they had never been friends, they had maintained a certain professional respect. But Ruth had detected an increase of hostility over the past weeks. She shrugged, then pulled the towel from her shoulders. It couldn't be helped. They were all there to dance.

"Ruth."

She jolted and spun around at the sound of Nick's voice. His eyes were cool on her face, without expression. A wave of anxiety washed over her. He was the cruelest when he controlled his temper. She had been in the wrong and was now prepared to admit it. "Nick," Ruth began, ready to humble herself with an apology.

"Go home."

She blinked at him, confused. "What?"

"Go home," he repeated in the same frigid tone.

Her eyes were suddenly round and eloquent. "Oh, no, Nick, I—"

"I said go." His words fell like an axe. "I don't want you here."

Even as she stared at him, she paled from the hurt. There was nothing, nothing he could have done to wound her more deeply than to send her away. She felt both a rush of angry words and a rush of tears back up in her throat. Refusing to give way to either, she turned and crossed the room. Picking up her bag, Ruth walked to the door.

"Second dancers, please," she heard Nick call out before she shut it behind her.

Ruth slept for three hours with Nijinsky curled into the small of her back. She had closed the blinds in her bedroom, and fresh from a shower, lay across the spread. The room was dim, and the only sound was the cat's gentle snoring. When she woke, she woke instantly and rolled from her stomach to her back. Nijinsky was disturbed enough to pad down to the foot of the bed. Huffily, he began to clean himself.

Nick's words had been the last thing she had thought of before her slumber and the first to play in her mind when she awoke. She had been wrong. She had been punished. No one she knew could be more casually cruel than Nikolai Davidov. She rose briskly to open the blinds, determined to put the afternoon's events behind her.

"We can't lie around in the dark all day," she informed Nijinsky, then flopped back on the bed to ruffle his fur. He pretended to be indignant but allowed her to fondle and stroke. At last, deciding to forgive her, he nudged his forehead against hers. The gesture brought Nick hurtling back into Ruth's mind.

"Why do you like him so much?" she demanded of Nijinsky, tilting his head until the unblinking amber eyes were on hers. "What is it about him that attracts you?" Her brows lowered, and she began to scratch under the cat's chin absently as she stared into the distance. "Is it his voice, that musical, appealingly accented voice? Or is it the way he moves, with such fluidly controlled grace? Or how he smiles, throwing his whole self into it? Is it how he touches you, with his hands so sure, so knowing?"

Ruth's mind drifted back to the evening before, when Nick had stood holding her naked in his arms. For the first time since the impulsive, arousing kiss, Ruth allowed herself to think of it. The night before, she had dressed in a frenzy and had rushed off to the party with Donald, not giving herself a chance to think. She had come home exhausted and had fought with fatigue all day. Now rested, her mind clear, she dwelled on the matter of Nick Davidov. There was no question: She had seen desire in his eyes. Ruth curled on the spread again, resting her cheek on her hand. He had wanted her.

Desire. Ruth rolled the word around in her mind. Is that what I saw in his eyes? The thought had warmth creeping under her skin. Then, like a splash of ice water, she remembered his eyes that afternoon. No desire, no anger, not even disapproval. Simply nothing.

For a moment Ruth buried her face in the spread. It still hurt to remember his dismissal of her. She felt as though she had been cast adrift. But her common sense told her that one botched rehearsal wasn't the end of the world, and one kiss, she reminded herself, wasn't the beginning of anything.

The poster on the far wall caught her eye. Her uncle had given it to her a decade before. Lindsay and Nick were reproduced in their roles as Romeo and Juliet. Without a second thought, Ruth reached over, picked up the phone and dialed.

"Hello." The voice was warm and clear.

"Lindsay."

"Ruth!" There was surprise in the voice, followed by a quick rush of affection. "I didn't expect to hear from you before the weekend. Did you get Justin's picture?"

"Yes." Ruth smiled, thinking of the boldly colored abstract her four-year-old cousin had sent to her. "It's beautiful."

"Naturally. It's a self-portrait." Lindsay laughed her warm, infectious laugh. "You've missed Seth, I'm afraid. He's just run into town."

"That's all right." Ruth's eyes were drawn back to the poster. "I really called just to talk to you."

There was only the briefest of pauses, but Ruth sensed Lindsay's quick understanding. "Trouble at rehearsal today?"

Ruth laughed. She tucked her legs under her. "Right. How did you know?"

"Nothing makes a dancer more miserable."

"Now I feel silly." Ruth gathered her hair in her hand and tossed it behind her back.

"Don't. Everyone has a bad day. Did Nick shout at you?" There was a trace of humor rather than sympathy; that in itself was a balm.

"No." Ruth glanced down at the small pattern of flowers in the bedspread. Thoughtfully, she traced one with her thumbnail. "It'd be so much easier if he had. He told me to go home."

"And you felt as though someone had knocked you down with a battering ram."

"And then ran me over with a truck." Ruth smiled into the phone. "I knew you'd understand. What made it worse, he was right."

"He usually is," Lindsay said dryly. "It's one of his less endearing traits."

"Lindsay . . ." Ruth hesitated, then plunged before she could change her mind. "When you were with the company, were you ever—attracted to Nick?"

Lindsay paused again, a bit longer than she had the first time. "Yes, of course. It's impossible not to be, really. He's the sort of man who draws people."

"Yes, but..." Ruth hesitated again, searching for the right words. "What I meant was—"

"I know what you meant," Lindsay said, sparing her. "And yes, I was once very attracted."

Ruth glanced back up at the poster again, studying the star-crossed lovers. She dropped her eyes. "You're closer to him, I think, than anyone else."

"Perhaps." Lindsay considered a moment, weighing Ruth's tone and her own choice of words. "Nick's a very private person."

Ruth nodded. The statement was accurate. Nick could give of himself to the company, at parties, to the press and to his audience. He could flatter the individual with personal attention, but he was amazingly reticent about his personal life. Yes, he was careful about who he let inside. Suddenly Ruth felt alone.

"Lindsay, please, will you and Uncle Seth come to the opening? I know it's difficult, with the children and the school and Uncle Seth's work, but... I need you."

"Of course," Lindsay agreed without hesitation, without questions. "We'll be there."

Hanging up a few moments later, Ruth sat in silence. I feel better, she decided, just talking to her, making contact. She's more than family, she's a dancer, too. And she knows Nick.

Lindsay had been a romantically lovely Juliet to Nick's Romeo. It was a ballet Ruth had never danced with him. Keil Lowell had been her Romeo; a dark whip of a dancer who loved practical jokes. Ruth had danced with Nick in *Don Quixote,* in *The Firebird* and in his ballet *Ariel,* but in her mind Juliet had remained Lindsay's role. Ruth had searched for one of her own. She believed she had found it in Carlotta of *The Red Rose.*

It was hers, she thought suddenly. And she had better not forget it. Jumping from the bed, she pulled tights from her dresser drawer and began to tug them on.

When Ruth entered the old, six-story building that housed the company, it was past seven, but there were still some members of the troupe milling about. Some hailed her, and she waved in return but didn't stop. Newer members of the *corps* watched her pass. *Someday,* they thought. Ruth might have felt their dreams rushing past her if she hadn't been so impatient to begin.

She took the elevator up, her mind already forming the moves she would demand of her body. She wanted to work.

She heard the music before she pushed open the door of the studio. It always seemed larger without the dancers. She stood silently by the door and watched.

Nikolai Davidov's leaps were like no one else's. He would spring as if propelled, then pause and hang impossibly suspended before descending. His body was as fluid as a waterfall, as taut as a bow string. He had only to command it. And there was more, Ruth knew, just as mesmerized by him as she had been the first time she'd seen him perform; there was his precision timing, his strength and endurance. And he could act—an essential part of ballet. His face was as expressive as his body.

Davidov was fiercely concentrating. His eyes were fixed on the mirrored wall as he searched for faults. He was perfecting, refining. Sweat trickled down his face despite the sweatband he wore. There was virility as well as poetry in his moves. Ruth could see the rippling, the tightening of muscles in his legs and arms as he threw himself into the air, twisting and turning his body, then landing with perfect control and precision.

Oh God, she thought, forgetting everything but sheer admiration. *He is magnificent.*

Nick stopped and swore. For a moment he scowled at himself in the glass, his mind on his own world. When he walked back to the cassette recorder to replay the tape, he spotted Ruth. His eyes drifted over her, touching on the bag she had slung over her shoulder.

"So, you've rested." It was a simple statement, without rancor.

"Yes." She took a deep breath as they continued to watch each other. "I'm sorry I wasn't any good this morning." When he didn't speak, she walked to a bench to change her shoes.

"So, now you come back to make up?" There was a hint of amusement in his voice.

"Don't make fun of me."

"Is that what I do?" The smile lingered at the corners of his mouth.

Her eyes were wide and vulnerable. She dropped them to the satin ribbons she crossed at her ankles. "Sometimes," she murmured.

He moved softly. Ruth wasn't aware he had come to her until he crouched down, resting his hands on her knees. "Ruth." His eyes were just below hers now, his tone gentle. "I don't make fun of you."

She sighed. "It's so difficult when you're so often right." She made a face at him. "I wasn't going to that silly party until you made me so mad."

"Ah." Nick grinned, squeezing her knee companionably. "So, it's my fault, then."

"I like it better when it's your fault." She pulled the towel from her bag and used it to dry his damp face. "You work too hard, Davidov," she said. Nick lifted his hands lightly to her wrists.

"Do you worry about me, *milaya?*"

His eyes were thoughtful on hers. They're so blue, Ruth thought, like the sea from a distance or the sky in summer. "I never have before," she mused aloud. "Wouldn't it be strange if I started now? I don't suppose you need anyone to worry about you."

He continued to look at her, then the smile slid into his eyes. "Still, it's a comfortable feeling, yes?"

"Nick." He had started to rise, but Ruth put a hand to his shoulder. She found herself speaking quickly while the courage was with her. "Last night—why did you kiss me?"

He lifted a brow at the question, and though his eyes never left hers, she felt the rest of her body grow warm from them. "Because I wanted to," he told her at length. "It's a good reason." He rose then, and she got up with him.

"But you never wanted to before."

The smile was quick, speeding across his face. "Didn't I?"

"Well, you never kissed me before, not like that." She turned away, pulling off the T-shirt she wore over her bone-colored leotard.

He studied the graceful arch of her back. "And do you think I should do everything I want?"

Ruth shrugged. She had come to dance, not to fence. "I imagined you did," she tossed back as she approached the barre. As she went into a deep *plié,* she cast a look back over her shoulder. "Don't you?"

He didn't smile. "Do you mean to be provocative, Ruth, or is it an accident?"

She sensed the irritation in his voice but shrugged again. Perhaps she did. "I haven't tried it very often before," she said carelessly. "It might be fun."

"Be careful where you step," he said quietly. "It's a long fall."

Ruth laughed, enjoying the smooth response of her muscles to her commands. "Being safe isn't my goal in life, Nikolai. You'd understand if you'd known my parents. I'm a born adventurer."

"There are different kinds of danger," he pointed out, moving back to the cassette. "You might not find them all pleasurable."

"Do you want me to be afraid of you?" she asked, turning.

The recorder squawked when he pressed the fast forward button. "You would be," he told her simply, "if it were what I wanted."

Their eyes met in the mirror. It took all of Ruth's concentration to complete the leg lift. *Yes,* she admitted silently, keeping her eyes on his. *I would be.* There's no emotion he can't rip from a person. That, along with his technical brilliance, makes him a great dancer. But I won't be intimidated. She dipped to the ground again, her back straight.

"I don't frighten easily, Nick." In the glass, her eyes challenged.

He pushed the button, stopping the machine. The room was thrown into silence while the last of the sun struggled into the window.

"Come." Nick again pressed a button on the recorder. Music swelled into the room. Walking to the center, Nick held out a hand. Ruth crossed to him, and without speaking they took their positions for the *grand pas de deux.*

Nick was not only a brilliant dancer, he was a demanding teacher. He would have each detail perfect, each minute gesture exact. Again and again they began the movement, and again and again he stopped to correct, to adjust.

"No, the head angle is wrong. Here." He moved her head with his hands until he was satisfied. "Your hands here, like so." And he would position her as he chose.

His hands were professional, adjusting her shoulders, skimming lightly at her waist as she spun, gripping her thigh for a lift. She was content to be molded by him. Yet it seemed she could not please him. He grew impatient, she frustrated.

"You must *look* at me!" he demanded, stopping her again.

"I was," she tossed back, frowning.

With a quick Russian oath he walked over and punched the button to stop the tape. "With no feeling! You feel nothing. It's no good."

"You keep stopping," she began.

"Because it's wrong."

She glared at him briefly. "All right," she muttered and wiped the sweat from her brow with her forearm. "What do you want me to feel?"

"You're in love with me." Ruth's eyes flew up, but he was already involved with the tape recorder. "You want me, but you have pride, spirit. You won't be taken, do you see? Equal terms or nothing." He turned back, his eyes locking on hers. "But the desire is there. Passion, Ruth. It smolders. *Feel* it. You tell me you're a woman, not a child. Show me, then."

He crossed back to her. "Now," he said, putting a hand to her waist. "Again."

This time Ruth allowed her imagination to move her. She was a gypsy in love with a prince, fiercely proud, deeply passionate. The music was fast, building the mood. It was an erotic dance, with a basic sexuality in the steps and gestures. There was a great deal of close work, bodies brushing, eyes locking. She felt the very real pull of desire. Her blood began to hum with it.

Eagerly, as if to burn out what she was feeling, she executed the *soubresauts* trapped somewhere between truth and fantasy. She did want him and was no longer sure that she was feeling only as Carlotta. He touched her, drew her, and always she retreated—not running away but simply standing on her own.

The music built. They spun further and further away from each other, each rejecting the attraction. They leaped apart, but then, as if unable to resist, they came back full circle. Back toward each other and past, then, with a final turn, they were in each other's arms. The music ended with the two wrapped close together, face to face, heart to heart.

The silence came as a shock, leaving Ruth dazed between herself and the role. Both she and Nick were breathing quickly from the demands of the dance. She could feel the rapid beat of his heart against hers. Her eyes, as she stood on point were almost level with his. He looked into hers as she did into his—searching, wondering. Their lips met; the time for questions was passed.

This time she felt the hunger and impatience she had only sensed before. He seemed unable to hold her close enough, unable to taste all he craved. His mouth was everywhere, running wildly over her face and throat. White heat raced along her skin in its wake. She could smell the muskiness of his sweat, taste the salty dampness on his face and throat as her own lips wandered. Then his mouth came back to hers, and they joined in mutual need.

He murmured something, but she couldn't understand. Even the language he spoke was a mystery. Their bodies fused together. Only the thin fabric of her leotard and tights came between his hands and her skin. They pressed here, touched there, lingered and aroused. His lips were at her ear, his teeth catching and tugging at the lobe. He murmured to her in Russian, but she had no need to understand the words.

His mouth found hers again, hotter this time, more insistent. Ruth gave and took with equal urgency, shuddering with pleasure as he slid a hand to her breast for a rough caress while her mouth, ever searching, ever questing, clung to his.

When he would have drawn her away, Ruth buried her face in his shoulder and strained against him. Nothing had ever prepared her for the rapid swing of strength to weakness. Even knowing she was losing part of herself, she was unable to stop it.

"Ruth." Nick drew her away, his hands gentle now. He looked at her, deep into the cloudy depths of her eyes. She was too moved by what was coursing through her to read his expression. "I didn't mean that to happen."

She stared at him. "But it did." It seemed so simple. She smiled. But when she lifted a hand to touch his cheek, he stopped her by taking her wrist.

"It shouldn't have."

She watched him, and her smile faded. Her eyes became guarded. "Why not?"

"We've a ballet to do in less than three weeks." Nick's voice was brisk now, all business. "This isn't the time for complications."

"Oh, I see." Ruth turned away so that he wouldn't see the hurt. Walking back to the bench, she began to untie her shoes. "I'm a complication."

"You are," he agreed and moved to the recorder again. "I haven't the time or the inclination to indulge you romantically."

"Indulge me romantically," she repeated in a low, incredulous voice.

"There are women who need a candlelight courtship," he continued, his back still to her. "You're one of them. At this point I haven't the time."

"Oh, I see. You only have time for more basic relationships," she said sharply, tying her tennis shoes with trembling fingers. How easily he could make her feel like a fool!

Nick turned to her now, watchful. "Yes."

"And there are other women who can provide that."

He gave a slight shrug. "Yes. I apologize for what happened. It's easy to get caught up in the dance."

"Oh, please." She tossed her toe shoes into the bag. "There's no need to apologize. I don't need you to indulge me romantically, Nick. Like you, I know others."

"Like your designer?"

"That's right. But don't worry, I won't blow any more rehearsals. I'll give you your ballet, Nick." Her voice was thickening with tears, but she was helpless to prevent it. "They'll rave about it, I swear it. It's going to make me the most important prima ballerina in the country." The tears came, and though she despised them, she didn't brush them aside. They rolled silently down her cheeks. "And when the season's over, I'll never dance with you again. *Never!*"

She turned and ran from the studio without giving him a chance to respond.

Chapter Four

The backstage cacophony penetrated Ruth's closed dressing room door. It was closed, uncharacteristically, for only one reason: She wanted to avoid Nick.

He was always everywhere before a performance—popping into dressing rooms, checking costumes and make-up, calming pre-performance jitters. No detail was too insignificant to merit his attention, no problem too small for him to seek the solution. He always had and always would involve himself.

In the past Ruth had cherished his brief, explosive visits. His energy was an inspiration and settled her own anxieties. Now, however, she wanted as much distance between herself and the company star and artistic director as possible. During the past weeks of rehearsal that hadn't been possible physically, but she would attempt an emotional distance nevertheless.

She felt reasonably certain that although Nick wouldn't normally respect a closed door, he would, in this case, take her point. The small gesture satisfied her.

Perhaps because of her turmoil and needs, Ruth had worked harder on the role of Carlotta than on any other role in her career. She was determined not just to make it a success, but to make it an unprecedented triumph. It was a gesture of defiance, a bid for independence. These days the character of the sultry gypsy suited her mood exactly.

In the three weeks since her last informal rehearsal with Nick, both dancers had kept their relationship stringently professional. It hadn't always been easy, given the roles they were portraying, but they had exchanged no personal comments, indulged in none of their usual banter. When she had felt his eyes follow her, as she had more than once, Ruth forced herself not to flinch. When she felt his desire draw her, she remembered his last private words to her. That had been enough to stiffen her pride. She had clamped down on her habit of speculating what was in his mind. She'd told herself she didn't need to know, didn't want to know. All she had to do was dance.

Now, dressed in a plain white terry robe, she sat at her dressing table and sewed the satin ribbons onto her toe shoes. The simple dancer's chore helped to relax her.

The heat of the bright, round bulbs that framed her mirror warmed her skin. Already in stage make-up, she had left her hair loose and thick. It was to fly around her in the first scene, as bold and alluring as her character. Her eyes had been darkened, accentuating their shape and size, her lips painted red. The brilliantly colored, full-skirted dress for the first scene hung on the back of the door. Flowers had already begun to arrive, and the room was heavy with scent. On the table at her elbow were a dozen long-stemmed red roses from Donald. She smiled a little, thinking he would be in the audience, then at the reception afterward. She'd keep his roses in her dressing room for as long as they lived. They would help her to remember that not all men were too busy to indulge her romantically.

Ruth pricked her finger on the needle and swore. Even as she brought the wound to her mouth to ease the sting, she caught the glare of her own eyes in the glass.

Serves you right, she told herself silently, for even thinking of him. Indulging her romantically indeed! She picked up her second toe shoe. He made me sound as though I were sixteen and needed a corsage for the prom!

Her thoughts were interrupted by a knock on the door. Ruth put down her shoe. She rose and went to the door. If it were Nick, she wanted to meet him on her feet. She lifted her chin as she turned the knob.

"Uncle Seth! Lindsay!" She launched herself into her uncle's arms, then flung herself at the woman beside him. "Oh, I'm so very glad you're here!"

Lindsay found the greeting a bit desperate but said nothing. She only returned the hug and met her husband's eyes over Ruth's head. Their communication was silent and perfectly understood. Ruth turned to give Seth a second hug.

"You both look wonderful!" she exclaimed as she drew them into the room.

Ruth had been close to Seth Bannion during much of her adolescence, but it hadn't been until she'd gone out on her own that she had truly appreciated the changes he had made in his own lifestyle to care for her. He was a highly successful architect and had been a sought-after bachelor and world traveler. He had taken a teen-ager into his home, adjusted his mode of living and made her his priority. Ruth adored him.

She clasped her hands and admired them both with her eyes. "You look so beautiful, Lindsay," Ruth enthused, turning to take her in. "I never get used to it." Lindsay was small and delicately built. Her pale hair and ivory skin set off her deep blue eyes. She was the warmest person Ruth knew; a woman capable of rich emotions and unlimited love. She wore a filmy smoke-gray dress that seemed to swirl from her shoulders to her feet.

Lindsay laughed and caught Ruth's hands in hers. "What a marvelous compliment. Seth doesn't tell me so nearly enough."

"Only daily," he said, smiling into Lindsay's eyes.

"This is the same dressing room you used for *Ariel*," Seth commented, glancing around. "It hasn't changed."

"You should know," Lindsay said. "I proposed to you here."

He grinned. "So you did."

"I didn't know that."

They both turned, shifting their attention to Ruth. Lindsay laughed again. "I've never been very good about tradition," she said and wandered over to pick up one of Ruth's toe shoes. "And he didn't ask me soon enough."

The shoes that lined the dressing table stirred memories. What a life, Lindsay thought. *What a world.* She had once been as much a part of it as Ruth was now. Her eyes lifted and fixed on the dark ones reflected in the glass.

"Nervous?"

Ruth's whole body seemed to sigh. "Oh, yes." She grimaced.

"It's a good ballet," Lindsay said with certainty. She took the quality of Nick's work on faith. She had known him for too long to do otherwise.

"It's wonderful. But..." Ruth shook her head and moved back to her chair. "In the second act there's a passage where I never seem to stop. There are only a few seconds for me to catch my breath before I'm off again."

"Nick doesn't write easy ballets."

"No." Ruth picked up her needle and thread again. "How are the children?"

The quick change of subject was noted. Again Lindsay met Seth's eyes over Ruth's head.

"Justin's a terror," Seth stated wryly with fatherly pride. "He drives Worth mad."

Ruth gave a low, gurgling laugh. "Is Worth maintaining his professional dignity?"

"Magnificently," Lindsay put in. "'Master Justin,'" she quoted, giving a fair imitation of the butler's cultured British tones. "'One must not bring one's pet frog into the kitchen, even when it requires feeding.'" Lindsay laughed, watching Ruth finish the last stitches. "Of course, he dotes on Amanda, though he pretends not to."

"And she's as big a terror as Justin!" Seth commented.

"What a way to describe our children," Lindsay said, turning to him.

"Who dumped the entire contents of a box of fish food into the goldfish bowl?" he asked her, and she lifted a brow.

"She was only trying to be helpful." A smile tugged at Lindsay's mouth. "Who took them to the zoo and stuffed them with hot dogs and caramel corn?"

"I was only trying to be helpful," he countered, his eyes warm on hers.

Watching them, Ruth felt both a surge of warmth and a shaft of envy. What would it be like to be loved that way? she wondered. *Enduringly.* The word suited them, she decided.

"Shall we clear out?" Lindsay asked her. "And let you get ready?"

"No, please stay awhile. There's time." Ruth fingered the satin ribbons nervously.

Nerves, Lindsay thought, watching her.

"You're coming to the reception, aren't you?" Ruth glanced up again.

"Wouldn't miss it." Lindsay moved over to knead Ruth's shoulders. "Will we meet Donald?"

"Donald?" Ruth brought her thoughts back. "Oh, yes, Donald will be there. Shall we get a table together? You'll like him," she went on without waiting for an answer. Her eyes sought Lindsay's, then her uncle's. "He's very—nice."

"Lindsay!"

Nick stood in the open doorway. His face was alive with pleasure. His eyes were all for Lindsay. She ran into his arms.

"Oh, Nick, it's wonderful to see you! It's always too long."

He kissed her on both cheeks, then on the mouth. "More beautiful every time," he murmured, letting his eyes roam her face. *"Ptichka,* little bird." He used his pet name for her, then kissed her again. "This architect you married"—he shot a quick grin at Seth— "he makes you happy still?"

"He'll do." Lindsay hugged Nick again fiercely. "Oh, but I miss you. Why don't you come see us more often?"

"When would I find the time?" He kept his arm around Lindsay's waist as he held out a hand to Seth. "Marriage agrees with you. It's good to see you."

Their handshake was warm. Seth knew he shared the two women he loved with the Russian. A part of Lindsay had belonged to Nick before he had known her. Now Ruth was part of his world.

"Are you giving us another triumph tonight?" Seth asked.

"But of course." Nick grinned and shrugged. "It is what I do."

Lindsay gave Nick a squeeze. "He never changes." She rested her head on his shoulder a moment. "Thank God."

Throughout the exchange, Ruth said nothing. She observed something rare and special between Lindsay and Nick. It emanated from them so vividly, she felt she could almost touch it. It only took seeing them side by side to remember how perfectly they had moved together on the stage. Unity, precision, understanding. She stopped listening to what they were saying, entranced by their unspoken rapport.

When Nick's eyes met hers, Ruth could only stare. Whatever she had been trying to dissect, to absorb, was forgotten. All she knew was that she had unwittingly allowed the ache to return. His eyes were so blue, so powerful, she seemed unable to prevent him from peeling away the layers and reaching her soul. Marshalling her strength, she pulled herself out of the trance.

It would have been impossible not to have witnessed the brief exchange. Lindsay and Seth silently communicated their concern.

"Nadine will be at the reception, won't she?" Lindsay attempted to ease the sudden tension.

"*Hmm?*" Nick turned his attention back to her. "Ah, yes, Nadine." He realigned his thoughts and spoke smoothly. "Of course, she will want to bask in the glory before she launches her next fund drive."

"You always were hard on her." Lindsay smiled, remembering how often Nick and Nadine Rothchild, founder of the company, had disagreed.

"She can take it," he tossed off with a jerk of his shoulder. "I'll see you at the reception?"

"Yes." Lindsay watched his eyes drift back to Ruth's. He hadn't spoken a word to her, nor had Ruth said anything to him. They communicated with their eyes only. He held the contact for several long seconds before turning back to Lindsay.

"I'll see you after the performance," he said, and Ruth quietly let out her breath. "I must go change. *Do svidanya.*"

He was gone before they could answer his good-bye. From down the corridor, they could hear someone calling his name.

Seth walked to Ruth and, putting his hands on her shoulders, bent to kiss the crown of her head. "You'd better be changing."

Ruth tried to pull herself together. "Yes, I'm in the first scene."

"You're going to be terrific." He squeezed her shoulders briefly.

"I want to be." Her eyes lifted to his and held before sweeping to Lindsay. "I have to be."

"You will be," Lindsay assured her, holding out a hand for Seth's even as her eyes stayed on Ruth's. "It's what you were born for. Besides, you were my most gifted pupil."

Ruth turned in the chair and gave Lindsay her first smile since Nick's appearance. She lifted her face to Lindsay's quick kiss. *"Do svidanya!"* Lindsay said, smiling as she and Seth left arm in arm.

Slowly Ruth moved to the door and shut it. For a moment she simply stood, contemplating the colorful costume that would make her Carlotta. She was Ruth

Bannion, a little unsure of her emotions, a little afraid of the night ahead. To put on the costume was to put on the role. Carlotta has her vulnerabilities, Ruth mused, fingering the fabric of the skirt, but she cloaks them in boldness and audaciousness. The thought made Ruth smile again. *Oh yes,* she decided, *she's for me.* Ruth began to dress.

When she left the room fifteen minutes later, she could hear the orchestra tuning up. She was in full costume. Her skirt swayed saucily at her hips, a slash of a red scarf defined her waist. Her hair streamed freely down her back. She hurried past the dancers warming up for the first scene and those idling in the doorways. She spotted Francie sitting cross-legged on the floor in a corner, breaking in her toe shoes with a hammer.

Ruth went to a convenient prop crate and used it for a barre as she began to warm up. She could already smell the sweat and the lights.

Her muscles responded, tightening, stretching, loosening at her command. She concentrated on them purposefully, keeping her back to the stage, the better to concentrate on her own body. Each performance was important to her, but this one was in a class by itself. Ruth had something to prove—to Nick and to herself. She would flaunt her professionalism. Whatever her feelings were for Nick, she would forget them and concentrate only on interpreting Nick's ballet. Nothing would interfere with that.

It had been a bad moment for her in the dressing room when his eyes had pinned hers. Something inside her had wanted to melt, and nearly had. Pride had held her aloof, as it had for weeks. He hadn't wanted her—not wholly, not exclusively—the way she had wanted him. The fact that he had so easily agreed that any number of women could give him what he needed had stung.

Scowling, Ruth curled her leg up behind her, pulling and stretching.

It was time someone taught that arrogant Russian a lesson, she thought as she switched legs. Too many women had fallen at his feet. He expected it, just as he expected his dancers to do things his way.

Ruth lifted her chin and found her eyes once again locked tight on Nick's.

He had come out of his dressing room clad in the glittering white and gold tunic he would wear in the first act. Spotting Ruth, he had stopped to stand and watch her. He wondered if the passion he saw in her face was her own or, like the costume, assumed for her role as Carlotta. He thought that there, in the dim backstage corridor, with the gypsy costume and smoldering eyes, she had never looked more alluring. It was at that moment that Ruth had lifted her eyes to his.

Each felt the instant attraction; each felt the instant hostility. Ruth tossed her head, glared briefly, then whirled away in a flurry of color and skirts. Her unconscious mimicry of the character she was about to play amused him.

All right, little one, Nick thought with the ghost of a smile. We'll see who comes out on top tonight. Nick decided he would rather enjoy the challenge.

He followed Ruth to the wings, dismissing with a wave of his hand one or two who tried to detain him. Reaching Ruth, he spun her around and caught her close, heedless of the backstage audience. She was caught completely off guard. Her reflexes had no time to respond or to reject before his mouth, arrogant and sure, demanded, plundered, then released.

Nick kept his hands on her forearms for a moment, arrogantly smiling. "That should put you in the mood," he said jauntily before turning to stride away.

Furious, Ruth could only stare hotly after his retreating back. There was scattered laughter that her glare did nothing to suppress before she whirled away again and stalked out onto the empty, black stage.

She waited while the stage hands drew the heavy curtain. She waited for the orchestra—strings only, as they played her entrance cue. She waited until she was fully lighted by the single spot before she began to dance.

Her opening solo was short, fast and flamboyant. When she had finished, the stage was lit to show the set of a gypsy camp. The audience exploded into applause.

While the *corps* and second dancers took over, Ruth was able to catch her breath. She waited, half-listening to the praise of Nick's assistant choreographer. Across the long stage she could see Nick waiting in the opposite wing for his entrance.

Top that, Davidov, she challenged silently. Ruth knew she had never danced better in her life. As if he had heard the unspoken dare, Nick grinned at her before he made his entrance.

He was all arrogance, all pride; the prince entering the gypsy camp to buy baubles. He cast aside the trinkets they offered with a flick of the wrist. He dominated the stage with his presence, his talent. Ruth couldn't deny it. It made her only more determined to outdo him. She waited while he dismissed offer after offer, waited for him to make it plain that the gypsies had nothing he desired. Then she glided on stage, her head held high. A red rose was now pinned at her ear.

Their mutual attraction was instant as their eyes met for the first time. The moment was accentuated by the change of lighting and the orchestra's crescendo. Carlotta, seeing the discarded treasures, turned her back on him to join a group of her sisters. The prince, intrigued, approached her for a closer study.

Ruth's mutinous eyes met Nick's again, and she had no trouble jerking her head haughtily away when he took her chin in his hand. Something in Nick's smile made her eyes flare more dramatically as he turned to the dancer who played her father. The prince had found something he desired. He offered his gold for Carlotta.

She defied him with pride and fury. No one could buy her; no one could own her. Taunting him, arousing him, she agreed to sell him a dance for his bag of gold. Enraged yet unable to resist, the prince tossed the gold onto the pile of rejected trinkets. They began their first *pas de deux,* palm to palm, with heated blood and angry eyes.

The high-level pace was maintained throughout the ballet. The competition between them remained sharp, each spurring the other to excel. They didn't speak between acts, but once, as they danced close, he whispered annoyingly in her ear that her *ballottés* needed polishing.

He lifted her, and she dipped, her head arched down, her feet up, so that he was holding her nearly upside down. Six, seven, eight slow, sustained beats, then she was up like lightning again in an *arabesque.* Her eyes were like flame as she executed a double turn. When she leaped offstage leaving him to his solo, Ruth pressed her hand to her stomach, drawing exhausted breaths.

Again and again, the stage burned from their heated dancing. When the ballet finally ended, the two in each other's arms, she managed to pant: "I dislike you intensely, Davidov."

"Dislike all you please," he said lightly as applause and cheers erupted. "As long as you dance."

"Oh, I'll dance, all right," she assured him breathlessly and dipped into a deep, smiling curtsy for the audience.

Only she could have heard his quiet chuckle as he scooped up a rose that had been tossed onstage and presented it to her with a bow.

"My *ballottés* were perfect," she hissed between gritted teeth as he kissed her hand.

"We'll discuss it in class tomorrow." He bowed and presented her to the audience again.

"Go to hell, Davidov," she said, smiling sweetly to the "bravos" that showered over them.

"After the season," he agreed, turning for another bow.

Chapter Five

Nick and Ruth took eleven curtain calls. An hour after the final curtain came down, her dressing room was finally cleared so that she could change from her costume. Now she wore a long white dress with narrow sleeves and a high collar. The only jewelry she added were the sleek gold drop earrings that Lindsay and Seth had given her on her twenty-first birthday. Triumph had made her eyes dark and brilliant and had shot a flush of rose into her cheeks. She left her hair loose and free, as Carlotta's had been.

"Very nice," Donald commented when she met him in the corridor.

Ruth smiled, knowing he spoke of the dress, his design, as much as the woman in it. She slipped her arm through his. "Like it?" Her eyes beamed up into his. "I found it in this little discount dress shop in the clothing district."

He pinched her chin as punishment, then kissed her. "I know I said it before, darling, but you were wonderful."

"Oh, I could never hear that too often." With a laugh she began to lead the way to the stage door. "I want champagne," she told him. "Gallons of it. I think I could swim in it tonight."

"Let's see if it can be arranged."

They moved outside, where his car was waiting. "Oh, Donald," Ruth continued, the moment they had settled into it. "It never felt more *right*. Everything just seemed to come together. The music—the music was so perfect."

"You were perfect," he stated, steering the car into Manhattan traffic. "They were ready to tear the walls down for you."

Much too excited to lean back, Ruth sat on the edge of her seat and turned toward him. "If I could freeze a moment in time, with all its feelings and emotions, it would be this ballet. Tonight. Opening night."

"You'll do it again tomorrow," he told her.

"Yes, and it will be wonderful, I know. But not like this." Ruth wished he could understand. "I'm not sure it can ever be exactly like this again, or even if it should be."

"I'd think you might get a bit weary of doing the same dance night after night after a couple of weeks."

He pulled over to the curb, and Ruth shook her head. Why did she want him to understand? she wondered as the doorman helped her alight. For all his creative talents as a designer, Donald was firmly rooted to the earth. But tonight she was ready to fly.

"It's hard to explain." She allowed him to lead her through the wide glass doors and into the hotel lobby. "Something just happens when the lights come on and the music starts. It's always special. Always."

The banquet room was ablaze with light and already crowded with people. Cameras began to click and flash the moment Ruth stepped into the doorway. The applause met her.

"Ruth!" Nadine walked through the crowd with the assurance of a woman who knew people would step aside for her. She was small, with a trim build and grace that revealed her training as a dancer. Her hair was sculptured and palely blond, her skin smooth and pink. The angelic face belied a keen mind. More than she ever had as a dancer, Nadine Rothchild, as company founder, devoted her life to the ballet.

Ruth turned to find herself embraced. "You were beautiful," Nadine said. Ruth knew this to be her highest compliment. Pulling her away, Nadine stared for several long seconds directly into her eyes. It was a characteristic habit. "You've never danced better than you danced tonight."

"Thank you, Nadine."

"I know you want Lindsay and Seth." She began to lead Ruth across the room, leaving Donald to follow in her wake. "We're all sitting together."

Ruth's eyes met Lindsay's first. What she read there was the final gratification. Lindsay held out both her hands, and Ruth extended hers to join them. "I'm so proud of you." Her voice was thick with emotion.

Seth laid his hands on his wife's shoulders and looked at his niece. "Every time I watch you perform, I think you'll never dance any better than you do at that moment. But you always do."

Ruth laughed, still gliding, and lifted her face for a kiss. "It's the most wonderful part I've ever had." She turned then, and taking Donald's arm, made quick introductions.

"I'm a great admirer of your designs." Lindsay smiled up at him. "Ruth wears them beautifully."

"My favorite client. I believe you could easily become my second favorite," Donald returned the compliment. "You have fantastic coloring."

"Thank you." Lindsay recognized the professional tone of the compliment and was more amused than flattered. "You need some champagne," she said, turning to Ruth.

Before they could locate a waiter, the sound of applause had them turning back toward the entrance. Ruth knew before she saw him that it would be Nick. Only he could generate such excitement. He was alone, which surprised her. Where there was Davidov, there were usually women. Ruth knew his eyes would find hers.

Nick quickly dislodged himself from the crowd and slowly, with the perfectly controlled grace of his profession, walked to her, holding a single red rose, which he handed to Ruth. When she accepted it, he took her other hand and lifted it to his lips. He didn't speak, nor did his eyes leave hers, until he turned and walked away.

Just theatrics, she told herself, but she couldn't resist breathing in the scent of the rose. No one knew how to set the stage more expertly than Davidov. Her eyes shifted to Lindsay's. In them Ruth could read both understanding and concern. She barely prevented herself from shaking her head in denial. She forced a bright smile.

"What about that champagne?" she demanded.

Ruth toyed with her dinner, barely eating, too excited for food. It was just as well; she sat at the table with Nadine, and it was a company joke that Nadine judged her dancers by the pound.

Nadine gave Lindsay's dish of chocolate mousse a frowning glance. "You have to watch those rich desserts, dear."

With a laugh Lindsay leaned over and kissed Nadine's cheek. "You're so wonderfully consistent, Nadine. There's too much in the world that's unpredictable."

"You can't dance with whipped cream in your thighs," Nadine pointed out and sipped at her champagne.

"You know," Lindsay said to Ruth, "she caught me once with a bag of potato chips. It was one of the most dreadful experiences of my life." She shot Nadine a grin and licked chocolate from her spoon. "It completely killed my taste for them."

"My dancers look like dancers," Nadine said firmly. "Lots of bone and no bulges. Proper diet is as essential as daily class—"

"And daily class is as essential as breathing," Lindsay finished and laughed again. "Can it really be eight years since I was with the company?"

"You left a hole. It wasn't easy to fill it."

The unexpected compliment surprised Lindsay. Nadine was a pragmatic, brisk woman who took her dancers' talent for granted. She expected the best and rarely considered praise necessary.

"Why, thank you, Nadine."

"It wasn't a compliment but a complaint," Nadine countered. "You left us too soon. You could still be dancing."

Lindsay smiled again. "You seem to have plenty of young talent, Nadine. Your *corps* is still the best."

Nadine acknowledged this with a nod. "Of course." She paused a moment, looking at Lindsay again as she sipped her wine. "Can you imagine how many Juliets I've watched in my lifetime, Lindsay?"

"Is that a loaded question?" she countered and grinned at Seth. "If I say too many, she'll complain that I'm aging her. Too few, and I'm insulting her."

"Try 'a considerable number,' " he suggested, adding champagne to his wife's glass.

"Good idea." Lindsay shifted her attention back to Nadine. "A considerable number."

"Quite correct." Nadine set down her glass and laid her hands on Lindsay's. Her eyes were suddenly intense. "You were the best. The very best. I wept when you left us."

Lindsay opened her mouth, then shut it again on words that wouldn't come. She swallowed and shook her head.

"Excuse me, please," she murmured. Rising, she hurried across the room.

There were wide glass doors leading to a circling balcony. Lindsay opened them and stepped outside. Leaning on the rail, she took a deep breath. It was a clear night, with stars and moonlight shedding silver over Manhattan's skyline. She looked out blindly.

After all the years, she thought, and all the distance. I'd have cut off an arm to have heard her say that ten years ago. She felt a tear run down her cheek and closed her eyes. Oh, God, how badly I once needed to know what she just told me. And now . . .

At the touch of a hand on her shoulder, she started. Lindsay turned into Nick's arms. For a moment she said nothing, letting herself lean on him and remember. She had been his Juliet in that other life, that world she had once been a part of.

"Oh, Nick," she murmured. "How fragile we are, and how foolish."

"Foolish?" he repeated and kissed the top of her head. "Speak for yourself, *ptichka*. Davidov is never foolish."

She laughed and looked up at him. "I forgot."

"Foolish of you." He pulled her back into his arms, and she rose on her toes so that her cheek brushed his. "Nick. You know, no matter how long you're away, no matter how far you go, all of this is still with you. It's more than in your blood, it's in the flesh and muscle." With a sigh, she drew out of his arms and again leaned on the rail. "Whenever I come back, part of me expects to walk into class again or rush to make company calls. It's ingrained."

Nick rested a hip on the rail and studied her profile. There was a breeze blowing her hair back, and he thought again that she was one of the most beautiful women he had ever known. Yet she had always seemed unaware of her physical appeal.

"Do you miss it?" he asked her, and she turned to look at him directly.

"It's not a matter of missing it." Lindsay's brows drew together as she tried to translate emotion into words. "It's more like putting part of yourself in storage. To be honest, I don't think about the company much at home. I'm so busy with the children and my students. And Seth is..." She stopped, and he watched the smile illuminate her face. "Seth is everything." Lindsay turned back to the skyline. "Sometimes, when I come back here to watch Ruth dance, the memories are so vivid, it's almost unreal."

"It makes you sad?"

"A little," she admitted. "But it's a nice feeling all the same. When I look back, I don't think there's anything in my life I'd change. I'm very lucky. And Ruth..." She smiled again, gazing out at New York. "I'm proud of her, thrilled for her. She's so good. She's so incredibly good. Somehow I feel like a part of it all over again."

"You're always a part of it, Lindsay." He caught at the ends of her hair. "Talent like yours is never forgotten."

"Oh, no, no more compliments tonight." She gave a shaky laugh and shook her head. "That's what got me started." Taking a deep breath, she faced him again. "I know I was a good dancer, Nick. I worked hard to be. I treasure the years I was with your company—the ballets I danced with you. My mother still has her scrapbook, and one day my children will look through it." She gave him a puzzled smile. "Imagine that."

"Do you know, I'm always amazed to think of you with two growing children."

"Why?"

He smiled and took her hand. "Because it's so easy to remember you the first time I saw you. You were still a soloist when I came to the company. I watched you rehearsing for *Sleeping Beauty*. You were the flower fairy, and you were dissatisfied with your *fouettés*."

"How do you remember that?"

Nick lifted a brow. "Because my first thought was how I would get you into my bed. I couldn't ask you—my English was not so good in those days."

Lindsay gave a choked laugh. "You learned quickly enough, as I remember. Though as I recall, you never, in any language, suggested I come into your bed."

"Would you have?" He tilted his head as he studied her. "I've wondered for more than ten years."

Lindsay searched her heart even as she searched his face. She could hear laughter through the windows and the muffled drone of traffic far below. She tried to think of the Lindsay Dunne who had existed ten years before. Ultimately, she smiled and shook her head. "I don't know. Perhaps it's better that way."

Nick slipped an arm around her, and she leaned against his shoulder. "You're right. I'm not sure it would be good to know one way or the other."

They fell silent as their thoughts drifted.

"Donald Keyser seems like a nice man," Lindsay murmured. She felt the fractional stiffening of Nick's arm.

"Yes."

"Ruth's not in love with him, of course, but he isn't in love with her, either. I imagine they're good company for each other." When he said nothing, Lindsay tilted her head and looked at him. "Nick?"

He glanced down and read her unspoken thoughts clearly. "You see too much," he muttered.

"I know you—I know Ruth."

He frowned back out at the skyline. "You're afraid I'll hurt her."

"The thought has crossed my mind," Lindsay admitted. "As it crossed my mind that she might hurt you." Nick looked back at her, and she continued. "It's difficult when I love you both."

After a shrug, he thrust his hands deep into his pockets and turned to take a few steps away. "We dance together, that's all."

"That's hardly all," Lindsay countered, but as he turned back, annoyed, she continued. "Oh, I don't mean you're lovers, nor is it any of my business if you are. But Nick." She sighed, recognizing the anger in his eyes. "It's impossible to look at the two of you and not see."

"What do you want?" he demanded. "A promise I won't take her to bed?"

"No." Calmly, Lindsay walked to him. "I'm not asking for promises or giving advice. I only hope to give you support if you want it."

She watched the anger die as he turned away again. "She's a child," he murmured.

"She's a woman," Lindsay corrected. "Ruth was barely ever a child. She was grown up in a number of ways when I first met her."

"Perhaps it is safer if I consider her a child."

"You've argued with her."

Nick laughed and faced Lindsay again. "*Ptichka,* I always argue with my partners, yes?"

"Yes," Lindsay agreed and decided to leave it at that. Instead of pressing him, she held out her hand. "We had some great arguments, Davidov."

"The best." Nick took the offered hand in both of his. "Come, let me take you back in. We should be celebrating."

"Did I tell you how wonderful you were tonight or how brilliant your ballet is?"

"Only once." He gave her his charming smile. "And that was hardly enough. I have a very big ego." The creases in his cheeks deepened. "How wonderful was I?"

"Oh, Nick." Lindsay laughed and threw her arms around him. "As wonderful as Davidov can possibly be."

"A suitable compliment," he decided, "as that is a great deal more brilliant than anyone else."

Lindsay kissed him. "I'm so glad you don't change."

They both turned as the door opened. Seth stepped out on the balcony.

"Ah, we're caught," Nick stated, grinning as he kept Lindsay in his arms. "Now your architect will break both my legs."

"Perhaps if you beg for mercy," Lindsay told him, smiling over at Seth.

"Davidov beg for mercy?" Nick rolled his eyes and released her. "The woman is mad."

"Often," Seth agreed. "But I make allowances for it." Lindsay's hand slipped into his. "People are asking for you," he told Nick.

Nick nodded, casting a quick glance toward the dining room. "How long are you staying?"

"Just overnight," Seth answered.

"Then I will say good-bye now." He held out a hand to Seth. *"Do svidanya, priyatel."* He used the Russian term for friend. "You're a man to be envied. *Do svidanya, ptichka."*

"Good-bye, Nick." Lindsay watched him slip back into the dining room. She sighed.

"Feeling better?" Seth asked her.

"How well you know me," she murmured.

"How much I love you," he whispered as he pulled her into his arms.

"Seth. It's been a lovely evening."

"No regrets?"

Lindsay knew he spoke of her career, the choices she had made. "No. No regrets." She lifted her face and met his mouth with hers.

The kiss grew long and deep with a hint of hunger. She heard his quiet sound of pleasure as he drew her closer. Her arms slipped up around his back until her hands gripped his shoulders. It's always like the first time, she thought. Each time he kisses me, it's like the first.

"Seth," she murmured against his mouth as they changed the angle of the kiss. "I'm much, much too tired for a party tonight."

"Hmm." His lips moved to her ear. "It's been a long day. We should just slip up to our room and get some rest."

Lindsay gave a low laugh. "Good idea." She brought her lips teasingly back to his. "Maybe we could order a bottle of champagne—to toast the ballet."

"A magnum of champagne," Seth decided, drawing her back far enough to smile down into her face. "It was an excellent ballet, after all."

"Oh, yes." Lindsay cast an eye toward the doors that separated them from the crowd of people. She smiled back at her husband. "I don't think we should disturb the party, do you?"

"What party?" Seth asked. Taking her arm, he walked past the doors. "There's another set of doors on the east side."

Lindsay laughed. "Architects always know the most important things," she murmured.

Chapter Six

By the end of the first week, *The Red Rose* was an established success. The company played to a full house at every performance. Ruth read the reviews and knew it was the turning point of her career. She gave interviews and focused on promoting the ballet, the company and herself. It was a simple matter to engage herself in her work and in her success. It was not so simple to deal with her feelings when she danced, night after night, with Nick.

Ruth told herself they were Carlotta's feelings; that it was merely her own empathy with the role she played. To fall in love with Davidov was impossible.

He was absorbed with ballet. So was she. He was only interested in brief physical relationships. Should she decide to involve herself with a man, she wanted emotions—deep, lasting emotions. The example of her own parents and Lindsay and Seth had spoiled her for anything less. Nick was demanding and selfish and unreasonable—not qualities she looked for in a lover. He found her foolish and romantic.

She needed to remember that after each performance when her blood was pumping and the need for him was churning inside her. She needed to remind herself of it when she lay awake at night with her mind far too wide awake.

They met on stage almost exclusively, so that when they came together face to face, the temptation was strong to take on the roles of the characters they portrayed. Whenever Ruth found herself too close to losing Carlotta's identity or her distance from Nick, she reviewed his faults. She had plans for her life, both professionally and personally. She was aware that Nick was the one man who could interfere with them.

She considered herself both self-sufficient and independent. She had had to be, growing up without an established home and normal childhood routines. There had been no lasting playmates in her young years, and she had taught herself not to form sentimental attachments to the homes her parents had rented, for they had never been homes for long. Ruth's apartment in New York was the first place she had allowed herself to grow attached to. It was hers—paid for with money she earned, filled with the things that were important to her. In the year she had lived there, she had learned that she could make it on her own. She had confidence in herself as a woman and as a dancer. It infuriated her that Nick was the only person on earth who could make her feel insecure in either respect.

Professionally, he could either challenge or intimidate her by a choice of words or with a facial expression. And Ruth was well aware of the confusion he aroused in her as a woman.

The girlhood crush was long over. For years, her passions had been centered on dancing. The men she had dated had been companions, friends. Nick had been the *premier danseur,* a mentor, a professional partner. It seemed strange to her that her feelings for him could have changed and intensified so quickly.

Perhaps, she thought, it would be easier to fall in love with a stranger rather than be in the embarrassing position of being suddenly attracted to a man she had known and worked with for years. There was no escape from the constant daily contact.

If it had been just a matter of physical attraction, Ruth felt she could have handled it. But it was the emotional involvement that worried her. Her feelings for Nick were complex and deep. She admired him, was fascinated by him, enraged by him, and trusted him without reservation—professionally. Personally, she knew he could, by the sheer force of his personality, overwhelm and devour. She wasn't willing to be the victim. Love, she feared, meant dependence, and that meant a lack of control.

"How far away are you?"

Ruth spun around to see Francie standing in her dressing room doorway. "Oh, miles," she admitted. "Come on in and sit down."

"You seem to have been thinking deep thoughts," Francie commented.

Ruth began to brush her hair back into a ponytail. *"Mmm,"* she said noncommittally. "Wednesday's are the longest. Just the thought of doing two shows make my toes cramp."

"Seven curtain calls for a matinee isn't anything to sneeze at." Francie sank down on a handy chair. "Poor Nick is at this moment giving another interview to a reporter from *New Trends*."

Ruth gave a half-laugh as she tied her hair back with a leather strap. "He'll be absolutely charming, and his accent will get more and more incomprehensible."

"*Spasibo*," Thank you, Francie said. "One of my few Russian words."

"Where did you learn that?" Ruth turned to face her.

"Oh, I did a bit of Russian cramming a couple of years ago when I thought I might enchant Nick." Grinning, Francie reached in her pocket for a stick of gum. "It didn't work. He'd laugh and pat me on the head now and again. I had delusions of gypsy violins and wild passion." She lifted her shoulders and sighed. "Nick always seems to be occupied, if you know what I mean."

"Yes." Ruth looked at her searchingly. "I never knew you were—interested in Nick that way."

"Honey." Francie gave her a pitying smile. "What female over twelve wouldn't be? And we all know my track record." She laughed and stretched her arms to the ceiling. "I like men; I don't fight it." She dropped her arms into her lap. "I just ended my meaningful relationship with the dermatologist."

"Oh. I'm sorry."

"Don't be sorry. We had fun. I'm considering a new meaningful relationship with the actor I met last week.

He's Price Reynolds on *A New Breed.*" At Ruth's blank look, she elaborated. "The soap opera."

Ruth shook her head while a smile tugged at her mouth. "I haven't caught it."

"He's tall, with broad shoulders and dark, sleepy eyes. He might just be the one."

Ruth bit her bottom lip in thought. "How do you know when he is?" She met Francie's eyes again. "What makes you think he might be?"

"My palms sweat." She laughed at Ruth's incredulous face. "No, really, they do. Every time. It wouldn't work for you." Francie stopped smiling and leaned forward as she did when she became serious. "It wouldn't be enough for you to think a man *might* be the one. You'd have to *know* he was. I've been in love twice already this year. I was in love at least four or five times last year. How many times have you been in love?"

Ruth looked at her blankly. "Well, I..." Never, she realized. There had been no one.

"Don't look devastated." Francie popped back out of the chair with all the exuberance she showed on stage. "You've never been in love because there's only one meaning of the word for you. You'll know it when it happens." She laid a friendly hand on Ruth's shoulders. "That's going to be it. You're not insecure, like me. You know what you want, what you need. You're not willing to settle for anything less."

"Insecure?" Ruth gave her friend a puzzled smile. "I've never imagined you as insecure."

"I need someone to tell me I'm pretty, I'm clever, I'm loved. You don't." She took a breath. "When we were in the *corps,* you knew you weren't going to stay there. You never had any doubt." She smiled again. "And neither did anyone else. If you found a man who meant as much to you as dancing does, you'd have it all."

Ruth dropped her eyes. "But he'd have to feel the same about me."

"That's part of the risk. It's like pulling a muscle." Francie grinned again. "It hurts like crazy, but you don't stop dancing. You haven't pulled a muscle yet."

"You're a great one with analogies."

"I only philosophize on an empty stomach," Francie told her. "Want lunch?"

"I can't. I'm meeting Donald." Ruth picked up her watch from the dressing table. "And I'm already late."

"Have fun." Francie headed for the door. "George is picking me up after tonight's show. You can get a look at him."

"George?"

"George Middemeyer." Francie tossed a grin over her shoulder. "Doctor Price Reynolds. He's a neurosurgeon with a failing marriage and a conniving mistress who might be pregnant. Tune in tomorrow."

With that, she was gone. Ruth laughed and grabbed her purse.

The delicatessen where Ruth was to meet Donald was two blocks away. She hurried toward it. She was aware that she was ten minutes late and that Donald was habitually prompt. She had little enough time before she had to report back for company calls.

The rich, strong smells of corned beef and Kosher pickles greeted her the moment she opened the door. The deli wasn't crowded, as the lunch rush was over, but a few people lingered. Two old men played a slow-moving game of checkers at a far table littered with the remnants of their lunch.

Ruth's glance swept over them and found Donald sitting back in his chair, smoking. She walked lightly, with rippling, unconscious confidence through the rows of tiny tables. "I'm sorry, Donald, I know I'm late." She leaned over to give him a quick kiss before she sat. "Have you ordered?"

"No." He tapped his cigarette. "I waited for you."

Ruth lifted a brow. There was something underlying the casual words. Knowing Donald, she told herself to wait. Whatever he had to say he would say in his own time.

She glanced over as the rotund, white-aproned man behind the counter shuffled over to their table. "What'll ya have?"

"Fruit salad and tea, please," Ruth told him, giving him a smile.

"Whitefish and coffee." Donald didn't glance at him. The man gave a little snort before shuffling off again. Ruth grinned at his retreating back.

"Have you ever been in here at lunch time?" she asked Donald. "It's a madhouse. He has a boy helping out during the rush, but they both move at the same pace. *Adagio.*"

"I rarely eat in places like this," Donald commented, taking a last drag before crushing out his cigarette.

Again Ruth detected undercurrents but waited. "It's really all I have time for today, Donald. Today must be pretty frantic for you, too, with your fashion show and reception tonight." She settled her purse strap over the back of her chair, then leaned her elbows on the table. "Is everything going well?"

"It appears to be. Some last-minute mayhem, naturally. Temperamental disagreements between my senior cutter and my head seamstress." He shrugged. "The usual."

"But this show is quite important, isn't it?" She tilted her head at his offhand tone.

"Yes, it's important." He shot her a direct look. "That's why I wanted you there with me."

Ruth met the look but kept her silence as the food was set unceremoniously on the table in front of them. Deliberately, she picked up her spoon but left the salad untouched. "You know why I can't, Donald. We've already discussed it."

He spilled a generous spoonful of sugar into his black coffee. "I also know you've got an understudy. One missed performance wouldn't matter that much."

"An understudy is for serious problems. I can't take a night off because I want to go out on a date."

"It's not quite movies and pizza," he said crossly.

"I know that, Donald." Ruth sipped the tea. A light throbbing had begun behind her eyes. "I'd be there if I could."

"I didn't let you down on opening night."

"That's hardly fair." Ruth set down her cup. She could see by the cool, set look on his face that his mind was already made up. "If you'd had a show scheduled to conflict with mine, you wouldn't have missed it, and I wouldn't have expected you to."

"You're not willing to make adjustments for me or for my work."

Ruth thought of the parties and functions she had attended at his insistence. "I give you what I can, Donald. You knew my priorities when we started seeing each other."

Donald stopped stirring his coffee and set the spoon on the table. "It isn't enough," he said coldly. Ruth felt her stomach tighten. "I want you with me tonight."

Her brow lifted. "An ultimatum?"

"Yes."

"I'm sorry, Donald." Her voice was low but without apology. "I can't."

"You won't," he countered.

"It hardly matters which way you put it," she said wearily.

"I'll be taking Germaine to the showing tonight."

Ruth looked at him. His choice showed a certain shrewdness. His biggest competitor would probably be more useful to him than a dancer.

"I've taken her out a few times recently," he explained. "You've been busy."

"I see." Ruth's response was noncommittal, although his words hurt.

"You've been too self-absorbed lately. There's nothing for you in your life but ballet. You refuse to make room in it for me, for any man. You've a selfish streak, Ruth. Class after class after class, with rehearsals and performances thrown in. Dancing's all you have, all you want."

His words shocked her at first, then cut. Ruth fumbled behind her for her purse, but Donald caught her arm.

"I'm not finished." He held her firmly in her chair. "You stand in front of those mirrors for hours, and what do you see? A body that waits to be told what to do by a choreographer. How often do you move on your own, Ruth? How often do you feel anything that isn't programmed into you? What will you have when the dancing stops?"

"Please." She bit down hard on her lip, trying without success to stop the flow of tears. "That's enough."

He seemed to focus on her face all at once. On a sharp breath, Donald released her arm. "Damn it, Ruth, I'm sorry."

"No." Frantically shaking her head, she pushed her chair back and rose. "Don't say any more." In a flash, she darted out the door.

The steamy summer air struck her like a blast. For a moment she looked up and down the street, confused, before turning toward the studio.

She hurried past the sea of strangers. The barbs that Donald had aimed had struck home—struck deep. Was she just an automaton? An empty body waiting to be filled by the bid of choreographers and composers? Was that how people from the outside saw her— as a ballerina on a music box, pirouetting endlessly until the music stopped?

She wondered how much truth had been in his angry words. Bursting through the front door of the building, she headed straight for her dressing room.

Once inside, she closed the door and leaned back against it. She was shaking from head to foot. A few short remarks from Donald had dehumanized her. Ruth moved slowly to her mirror and switched on all the lights. With hard, searching eyes, she studied her face.

Had her love and devotion for dancing made her selfish and one-dimensional? Was she really unable to feel deeply for a man, to make a positive commitment?

Ruth pressed her hands to her cheeks. The skin was soft, smooth, the scent on her hands was feminine. *But was she?* Ruth could read the panic in her eyes. Where did the dancer end and the woman begin? She shook her head and turned away from her own image.

Too many mirrors, she thought suddenly. There were too many mirrors in her life, and she was no longer certain what they reflected. What would she be in a decade, when the dancer faced the twilight of her career? Would memories and clippings be all she had?

Closing her eyes, Ruth forced herself to take several long breaths. She had three hours until curtain.

There was no time to dwell on problems. She would look for the answers after the performance.

Deciding what she needed was the lunch that had been so recently pushed aside, Ruth went down to the canteen for tea and an apple. The simple familiarity of the place helped level her. There were complaints about strained muscles, impossible dance combinations, Nadine's tight purse strings and the uncertain state of the plumbing on the fourth floor. By the time she was back at her dressing room door, she was steadier.

"Ruth!"

She looked over her shoulder as she placed her hand on the knob.

"Hello, Leah." Ruth tried to drum up some enthusiasm upon seeing the elegant blond dancer.

"Your reviews are marvelous." Leah eased her way into the dressing room as Ruth opened the door and entered. Too well, she knew the blond's penchant for stirring up trouble. Ruth felt she had had her fair share for one day.

"Roses for the whole ballet," Ruth agreed, walking over to take a seat at her dressing table as Leah settled into a chair. "But I don't imagine you found ballet reviews in there." She let her eyes fall on the tabloid Leah had in her hand.

"You never know whose name's going to pop up in here." She smiled at Ruth, then began thumbing through the paper. "I just happened to see a friend of yours mentioned in here. Let's see now, where . . . ?" She trailed off as she scanned the print. "Oh, yes, here it is. 'Donald Keyser,'" she quoted, "'top designer, has been seen recently escorting his fiery-headed competitor, Germaine Jones. Apparently his interest in ballet has waned.'" Leah lifted her eyes, moving her lips into a sympathetic little smile. "Men are such pigs, aren't they?"

Ruth swallowed her temper. "Aren't they."

"And it's so demeaning to be dumped in print, too."

Ruth's spine snapped straight. Color flowed in, then out of her cheeks. "I was dumped in the flesh as well," she said with the calm of determination. "So it hardly matters."

"He was terribly good-looking," Leah commented, meticulously folding the paper. "Of course, someone else is bound to come along."

"Haven't I told you about the Texan?" Ruth surprised herself, but the blank, then curious expression on Leah's face was motivation enough to maintain the pretense.

"Texan? What Texan?"

"Oh, we've been keeping a low profile," Ruth ad-libbed airily. "He can't afford to have his name splashed around in print until the divorce is final. Just piles of money, you know, and his second wife's not being very cooperative." She managed a slow smile. "You wouldn't believe the settlement. He offered her the villa in southern Italy, but she's holding out for his art collection. French impressionists."

"I see." Leah narrowed her eyes to a feline slit. "Well, well, aren't you the quiet one."

"Like a sphinx."

"You'll have to be careful how much Nick finds out," Leah warned, then ran the tip of her tongue over her top lip. "He really detests nasty publicity. He'll want to be particularly careful now that he's finalizing plans for that big special on cable television."

"Special?" Ruth echoed.

"Didn't you know?" Leah looked pleased again. "Featuring the company, of course, and spotlighting the principal dancers. I'll do Aurora, naturally, probably the wedding scene. I believe Nick plans to do a *pas de deux* from *Le Corsaire,* and, of course, one from *The Red Rose.* He hasn't chosen his partners yet." She paused deliberately and smiled. "We have two full hours of air time. Nick's very excited about filling it." She slanted Ruth a glance. "Strange he hasn't mentioned it to you, but perhaps he thought you wouldn't be up to it after the strain of these last few weeks."

Leah rose to leave. "Don't worry, darling, he'll be making the announcement in a few days. I'm sure he'll use you somewhere." She dropped the paper into the chair. "Dance well," she said and left, closing the door quietly behind her.

Chapter Seven

Ruth sat staring at the closed door for several long minutes. How could Leah know about such an enormously important project and she be left in the dark? *Unless Nick intended to exclude her.*

She knew she and Nick were having their personal problems, but professionally... Professionally, she remembered, she had told him that after this run she'd never dance with him again. Ruth recalled her own words and knew she had meant them, at least at that moment. But did that mean she was not to be partnered by anyone else? Could Nick be so vindictive?

Ruth knew that she was a good dancer. Would Nick drop her for personal reasons? After all, she had threatened him. Ruth closed her eyes and tried to control the rising sickness in her stomach.

He had barely spoken to her since that night. Was this his way of punishing her for claiming not to want or need him as a partner? Would he let someone else dance Carlotta? The thought was more than Ruth could bear. Over and over she told herself she was a fool to allow herself to grow so attached to a part. Many other women would become Carlotta; she had simply been the first. Yet Ruth knew she had had a hand in creating the role as much as Nick had. She had put her soul into it.

Opening her eyes, Ruth looked directly at the copy of *Keyhole* that was left on the chair. Leah had done her work well, Ruth realized on a long breath. She had wanted to upset Ruth before the performance, and she had succeeded. Everything Donald had said—every feeling of doubt and inadequacy—had been reinforced. Now she feared that Nick would release her from the company when *The Red Rose*'s engagement was finished.

Ruth buried her face in her hands a moment and tried to push it all away. She had a performance to give; nothing could interfere with that. She was a dancer. That couldn't be taken from her.

Less than an hour later Ruth stepped out of her dressing room to warm up backstage. Still shaken, she tried to focus all her power of concentration on the role she was to portray. On another night she would have left Ruth Bannion behind in the dressing room. But not this time. Tonight Carlotta's free-spirited confidence and verve would be difficult to capture.

Ruth loosened her muscles automatically, trying to block out Donald's and Leah's words, but they continued to play through her thoughts.

The sounds of the orchestra tuning brought her back to the moment. It all felt wrong—the costume, the lights, the whine of strings as they were tested. She was cold, numb. She forgot the first movements of the ballet.

Nick came out of his dressing room. His eyes sought Ruth. It was a habitual practice of his, and it annoyed him. A sign of weakness in himself, however slight, irritated him. Ruth Bannion was becoming a weakness. She was as cool as autumn offstage and as sultry as summer on it. The transition was playing havoc with his nerves. He didn't care for it one bit.

It was difficult to deal with desire that would not abate even when she appeared to be indifferent to him, then challenged him to take her the moment she moved onstage. No woman had made him feel curb and spur at the same time before.

Nick could see the tension in her back, although he couldn't see her face. Her body spoke volumes. "Ruth."

Her already tense shoulders went rigid at the sound of his voice. Slowly, fighting to compose her features, she turned. Something flickered over his face before it became closed and still.

"What's wrong?"

"Nothing." Ruth hoped her voice sounded casual. She didn't flinch when he took her chin in his hand to study her face. Beneath the make-up her skin was pale, her eyes dark and miserable.

"Are you ill?" Had there been concern in his voice, she might have collapsed.

"No."

Nick gave her a long, thorough study before dropping his hand. "Then snap out of it. You have to dance in a moment. If you had a fight with your boyfriend, your tears have to wait."

He heard her sharp intake of breath, saw the simultaneous cloud of hurt in her eyes. "I'll dance, don't worry. No one you've got lined up to replace me will ever dance this part better."

Nick's gaze narrowed as he curled his fingers around her arm. "What are you talking about?"

"Don't." Ruth jerked her arm free. "I've had enough dumped on me tonight. I don't need any more." Her voice broke, and cursing herself, Ruth walked to the wings to wait for her cue. She took long, steadying breaths and forced as much as possible out of her mind.

Her opening dance did not go well. Ruth comforted herself, as she stood again in the wings, that only the sharpest eyes would have detected any flaws. Technically her moves had been perfect, but Ruth knew a dancer had to give more than body to the dance. Her mind and heart had not flowed with her. Her inability to give her best shook her all the more.

She made her second entrance and moments later was dancing with Nick.

"Put some life into it," he demanded in low tones as she spun in a double pirouette. He lifted her into an *arabesque*. "You dance like a robot."

"Isn't that what you want?" she hissed back. *Jeté, jeté, arabesque,* and she was back in his arms.

"Be angry," he murmured, lifting her again. "Hate me, but think of me. *Of me.*"

It was difficult to think of anything else. His eyes alone demanded it throughout the performance. Ruth's nerves were stretched to the breaking point by the last act. Emotions were churning inside her until she feared she would be physically sick. Never before had she prayed for a performance to end. Her head pounded desperately, but she fought to the finish. She sagged against Nick when the curtains closed.

"You said you weren't ill." He took her by the shoulders. Ruth shook her head. "Can you take curtain calls?"

"Yes. Yes, of course." She tried to pull out of his arms. He resisted her efforts, then, when her eyes lifted questioningly to his, he released her to take her hand.

The applause was muffled against the heavy curtain, but with a nod from Nick, the drape was lifted. The applause was thunderous. Ruth winced at the volume of noise. Again and again she made her curtsies, hanging onto the knowledge that the long day was almost at an end.

"Enough," Nick said curtly when the applause battered against the curtain yet again. He began to lead her offstage left.

"Nick," Ruth began, confused because her dressing room was in the opposite direction.

"Ms. Bannion is ill," he told the stage manager as they brushed past. "She goes home. She sees no one."

"Nick, I can't," Ruth protested. "I have to change."

"Later." He all but pushed her into the elevator. "We're going up to my office." He punched a button, and the doors slid shut. "We'll talk."

"I can't," Ruth began in rising panic. "I won't."

"You will. For now, be quiet. You're shaking."

Because she knew he wasn't above force to get his own way, Ruth subsided when the doors opened and he propelled her down the hall. The entire floor was dark and deserted. Without the least hesitation, he located the door to his office. Pushing her through, Nick flipped on the lights, then closed and locked the door. "Sit," he ordered shortly, then moved to a low, ornate cabinet.

Ruth had rarely been inside the room. It bespoke a different aspect of Nikolai Davidov, the dancer, the choreographer. This was his executive domain. Here he dealt with the rich, urging money from them to keep the company alive. Ruth could easily imagine him sitting behind the huge, old oak desk, radiating charm and coaxing dollars from patrons. Hadn't she heard Nadine state that Nick was as valuable to the company behind a desk as he was onstage?

Charm. Charisma. That generous, intimate smile that made it impossible to say no. Yes, it was a talent, just as double *tours en l'air* required talent. And style. What was talent without style? Davidov had an abundance of both.

Ruth glanced around the stately office with its old, tasteful furniture and fat, leather chairs. How many thousands of dollars had begun their journey in this office from silk-lined pockets to props, costumes and lights? What elegant balletomane had paid for the costume she was wearing at that moment?

"I said *sit*."

Nick's curt order broke into Ruth's thoughts. She turned, but before she could speak, she found herself being turned toward the sofa. The unarguable pressure on her shoulder convinced her to sit. A brandy snifter, a quarter full, was thrust into her hands.

"Drink." So saying, Nick moved back to the cabinet for his own brandy. When he was sitting next to her, Nick leaned back into the curve of the sofa arm and watched her. A lift of his brow repeated his order, and Ruth sipped at the brandy.

Silently, he continued to study her while he swirled his own. The quiet was absolute. Ruth drank again, focusing her entire concentration on a scar in the wood of his desk.

"So." The word brought her eyes flying back to his face. He kept his own on hers while he lifted his glass. "Tell me," he ordered.

"There's nothing to tell."

"Ruth." He glanced down at the liquor in his glass as if considering its vintage. "You know at times I am a patient man. This," he said and brought his eyes back to hers, "is not one of those times."

"I'm glad you clarified that." Ruth finished off the brandy recklessly, then set down the snifter. "Well, thanks for the drink." She hadn't even started to rise when his hand clamped over her wrist.

"Don't press your luck," he warned softly. He kept her prisoner while he leisurely sipped his drink. "Answers," he told her. "Now."

"May I have the question first, please?" Ruth kept her voice light, but her pulse betrayed her by beating fitfully against his fingers.

"What was wrong with you tonight?"

"I was a little off." She made an impatient move with her shoulders.

"Why?"

"It was a mood. I have them." She tried, without success, to free her arm. The ease with which he prevented this was infuriating. "Aren't I entitled to any privacy?" she demanded. "Any personal feelings?"

"Not when it interferes with your work."

"I can't dance on automatic." The passion she tried to control slipped into her voice. Her eyes flared with it. "No matter what anyone thinks. I'm not just a body that dances when someone plays the tune. Oh, let me go!" She tugged on her hand again. "I don't want to talk to you."

Ignoring this demand, Nick set down his glass. "Who puts these thoughts into your head?" He took her shoulders, keeping her facing him when she would have turned away. "Your designer?" Her expression gave her away even as she shook her head.

Nick swore quietly in Russian. He increased the pressure of his fingers. "Look at me," he demanded. "Don't you know nonsense when it falls on your ears?"

"He said I had no feelings," she said haltingly, trying to control the tears that thickened her voice and blurred her vision. "That my life, my emotions were all bound up in ballet and without it . . ." She trailed off and shook her head.

"What does he know?" Nick gave her a quick, exasperated shake. "He's not a dancer. How does he know what we feel? Does he know the difference between jumping and soaring?" There was another quick, concise oath. "He's jealous. He wants to cage you."

"He wants more than I've given him," Ruth countered. "He's entitled to more. I do care about him, but—" She pushed her hair back from her face with both hands.

"You're not in love with him," Nick finished.

"No. No, I'm not. Maybe I'm just not capable of that kind of feeling. Maybe he's right, and I—"

"Stop!" He shook her again, harder than before. Springing up, he prowled the room. Ruth heard him muttering in Russian as he paced. "You're a fool to let anyone make you believe such things. Because you are not in love with a man, you let him convince you you're less than a woman?" He made a sound of disgust and whirled back to her. "What's wrong with you? Where's your spirit? Your temper? If I had said such things to you, you wouldn't have allowed it!"

Ruth pressed her fingers to her temple and tried to rearrange her thoughts. "But you would never have said those things to me."

"No." The answer was quiet. Nick walked back to her. "No, because I know you, understand what's in you. We have this, you see." He took her hand and laced their fingers. Ruth stared at the joined hands.

"You have your world and your designer has his. If there was love, you could live in both."

Ruth took a moment, carefully thinking over his words. "Yes, I'd want to," she said slowly. "I'd try to. But—"

"No. No buts. Buts tire me." He sank back down beside her, managing to make the inelegant movement graceful. "So you fought with your designer, and he said stupid things. Is this enough to make you pale and sick?"

"It didn't help to have my replacement shoved down my throat," Ruth shot back. "I didn't care for being taunted with a copy of *Keyhole* chatting about his new relationship an hour before curtain."

"*Keyhole?*" Nick frowned in confusion. "What is this *Keyhole?* Ah," he said, remembering before Ruth could elaborate. "The silly newspaper with the very bad pictures?"

"The silly newspaper that speculated Donald Keyser had lost interest in the ballet."

"Ah." Nick pressed his fingertips together. "He brought that by your dressing room?"

"No, not Donald..." Ruth broke off, alerted by the sharpening of his eyes. Quickly, she moistened her lips and rose. "It doesn't matter; it was stupid to let it upset me."

"Stop." The quiet order froze her. "Who?" Ruth felt the warning feather up her spine. "Who brought the paper to you before the performance?"

"Nick, I—"

"I asked you a question." He rose, too. "It's inexcusable for a member of the company to deliberately set out to disturb another before a performance. I do not permit it."

"I won't tell you. No, I won't," she added firmly as she saw the temper leap into his eyes. "I should've handled it better. I will next time. In any case, there was something more than Donald that upset me tonight." Ruth stood her ground, not so much wanting to protect Leah but more unwilling to subject anyone to the full force of Davidov's temper. She knew he could be brutal.

"I want a name."

"I won't give you one. I can't." She touched his arm and found the muscles rigid. "I just can't," she murmured, using what power she knew her eyes possessed. "There's something more important that we have to settle."

He became very still. Ruth searched his face, but his expression was guarded. Whatever his thoughts, they remained his alone. Feeling his withdrawal, Ruth took her hand from his arm.

"What?"

Ruth caught herself before she moistened her lips again. Her heart was beginning to pound furiously against her ribs. "I think I'd like another brandy first."

She waited for an angry, impatient refusal, but after a brief hesitation he picked up the snifters and went back to the liquor cabinet. The only sound was the splash of liquid as it hit the glass. She accepted the drink when he offered it, then sipped. She took a deep breath.

"Do you plan to release me from the company?"

Nick's own snifter paused on the way to his lips "What did you say?"

This time Ruth spoke more firmly. "I said, do you plan to release me from the company?"

"Do I look like a stupid man?" he demanded.

In spite of her tension, the incredulity in his tone made her smile. "No, Davidov."

"*Khorosho.* Good. For once, we agree." He flicked his wrist in angry confusion. "And since I am not a stupid man, why would I release from the company my finest ballerina?"

Ruth stared at him. Shock shot through her body and was plain on her face. "You never said that before," she whispered.

"Said what?"

Shaking her head, she pressed her fingers between her brows, then turned away. "As long as I can remember, I've wanted to dance." Ruth gave a muffled laugh as tears began to flow. "All these years, I've pushed myself—for myself, yes—for the dance and for you. And you never said anything like that to me before." She took a small, shuddering breath. "After a day like this, after tonight's performance, you stand there and very casually tell me I'm the finest ballerina you have." Ruth wiped tears away with a knuckle. "Only you, Nikolai, would choose such a time."

Though she hadn't heard him move, Ruth wasn't surprised when his hands touched her shoulders. "If

I hadn't said so before, I should have. But then, I haven't always considered words so very important.''

Nick ran his fingers through her hair, watching the light glint on it. "You're very important to me. I will not lose you."

Ruth felt her heart stop beating. Then, like thunder, it began to roar in her ears. We're only speaking of the company, she reminded herself. Of dancing only. She turned.

"Will you replace me as Carlotta for television?"

"For television?" he repeated. He struggled, as he had to do from time to time to think in precise English. "Do you mean the cable?" Reading the answer in her eyes, he continued. "But that is not yet finalized, how would you ... ?" He stopped. "So that's what you meant before you went on tonight. And this information, I imagine, came from the same person who brought you the little *Doorknob?*"

"*Keyhole,*" Ruth corrected, but he was swearing suddenly in what she recognized as full-blown Russian rage.

"This is not permitted. I will not have my dancers sniping at each other before a performance. I will tell you this: What plans I made, and what casting I do, *I* do." He glared at her, caught up in fury. "My decision. *Mine.* If I chose you to dance Carlotta, then you dance Carlotta."

"I said I wouldn't dance with you again," Ruth began. "But—"

"I care *that* for what you said," Nick told her with a snap of his fingers. "If I tell you to dance with me, then you do. You have no say in this."

His temper was in full swing, and Ruth's flared to match it. "I have a say in my own life."

"To go or stay, yes," he agreed. "But if you stay, you do as you're told."

"You haven't told me anything," she reminded him. "I have to hear of your big plans less than an hour before curtain. You've barely spoken to me in weeks."

"I've had nothing to say to you. I don't waste my time."

"You arrogant, insufferable pig! I've poured everything I have into this ballet. I've bled for it. If you think I'm going to let you hand it over to someone else without a fight, you *are* stupid. I don't care if it's a two-minute *pas de deux* or the whole ballet. It's mine!"

"You think so, little one?" His tone was deceptively gentle.

"I know so," she tossed back. "And don't call me little one. I'm a woman, and Carlotta's mine until I can't dance her anymore." She took a quick breath before continuing. "I'll be dancing her years after you're finished with Prince Stefan."

"Really?" He circled her throat with his hand and squeezed lightly. The meaning pierced through her fury. "And do you forget, *milaya*, who composed the ballet? Who choreographed it and cast you as Carlotta?"

"No. And don't you forget who danced it!"

"You have a lovely, slender neck," he murmured. His fingers caressed it. "Don't tempt me to break it."

"I'm too mad to be frightened of you, Davidov. I want a simple answer. Do I dance Carlotta on this special or not?"

His eyes roamed over her furious face. "I'll let you know. You've just under a week left in this run. We can discuss future plans when it's finished." He cocked a brow when she let out a furious sigh. "Incentive. Now you'll dance your heart out for me."

"You always know what to say, don't you, Nick?" Ruth started to turn away, but he stopped her.

Very slowly, very deliberately, he lowered his mouth until it hovered an inch above hers. After a long, breathless moment, his lips descended. He heard her draw in her breath at the contact. He could feel her pulse beat against his palm, but still he did not increase the pressure.

Caressingly, the tip of his tongue traced her lips until, with a quiet sigh, they parted and invited him to enter. He had never kissed her with such care before, with such aching tenderness. Was there a defense against such tenderness? Always before, there had been heat and fire and hints of fear. Now she felt nothing but mindless pleasure.

He nipped her bottom lip, stopping just before the point of pain, then he replaced his teeth with his tongue. There was a strong scent of stage makeup and sweat to mix with the taste of brandy. Weak and weightless, she let her head fall back, inviting his complete control.

Their lips clung a few seconds longer as he began to draw her away. Nick felt the quiet release of her breath as she opened heavy eyes to look at him. In them he saw that she was his. He had only to lower her to the couch or pull her to the floor. They were alone, she was willing. He could still taste her, a dark, wild honey flavor that taunted him.

"Little one," he murmured and slid his hand from her throat to stroke her cheek. "What have you eaten today?"

Ruth's thoughts were thrown into instant confusion. "Eaten?" she repeated dumbly.

"Yes, food." There was a hint of impatience in his voice as he scooped up his brandy again. "What food have you had today?"

"I..." Ruth's mind was a total blank. "I don't know," she said finally with a helpless gesture. Her body was still throbbing.

"When's the last time you had a steak?"

"A steak?" Ruth ran a hand through her hair. "Years," she decided with an exasperated laugh.

"Come, you need a good meal." He held out a hand. "I'll take you to dinner."

"Nick, I don't understand you." Bewildered, Ruth ignored his outstretched hand, but he took hers firmly in his and was soon pulling her toward the door. "Five minutes to change."

"Nick," Ruth stopped in the doorway to study him. "Will I ever understand you?"

His brows lifted and fell at the question. "I'm Davidov," he said with a quick grin. "Is that not enough?"

She laughed shakily. "Too much," she answered. "Too much..."

Chapter Eight

Dinner with Nick had been enjoyable but hardly il-
luminating. Looking back, Ruth realized that they
hadn't spoken of ballet at all. After a wild cab ride
home, which Nick had apparently enjoyed, he had
deposited her at her door with a very quick, passion-
less kiss.

Ruth had slept until the ring of her alarm clock the
following morning. Emotional exhaustion and rich
food had proven an excellent tranquilizer.

The next day, routine had taken over. Though her
mind still fretted for answers, Ruth knew Nick well
enough to realize he intended to make her wait for
them. The more she pressed, the more reticent he became.

As the two-week run of *The Red Rose* came to an
end, Ruth dealt with the familiar let-down feeling that
came with the completion of an engagement. She
would be in limbo for a time, waiting for Nick to as-
sign her another role. It was one more unanswered
question.

Ruth hung up Carlotta's costume on closing night
and felt as though she was losing part of herself. She
was in no mood to go to the cast party, though she
knew she should at least put in an appearance.

I'd be lousy company, she told herself with a wry smile. No champagne tonight, she decided quickly as she creamed off her makeup. Just a huge glass of milk and an entire bag of cookies, all to myself. No one to share them with but Nijinsky. Ruth pulled on jeans. No brooding, just gorging.

"Come on in!" she called out when there was a knock on her door. She pulled a T-shirt down over her hips as Francie popped her head in.

"Where are you hiding?" she demanded. "They're already into the champagne."

"I'm skipping out," Ruth told her, picking up her purse.

"Oh, but you can't." Francie was still in full costume and make-up. Her darkened lips pouted. "I want you to meet my neurosurgeon."

"Can't tonight." Ruth shot her a grin and a wink. "Big plans."

"Oh?" Francie drew out the word knowingly. "Why didn't you bring him by?"

"I'm not sharing him with anyone," she told her. She let out a big anticipatory sigh. "All mine."

"Wow." Francie's brows shot up. "What's he like?"

"Delicious." Ruth couldn't resist as she swung through the door. "Absolutely delicious."

"Have I seen him?" Francie called out, but Ruth just laughed and dashed for the stage door.

Two hours later Ruth sat in a living room chair. Nijinsky lay sprawled at her feet, belly up, his front paws posed like a fighter's, ready to lead with the left.

Ruth yawned. The old movie on TV wasn't holding her attention. Still she was glad she had slipped out on the party. Her mood had been wrong. The crowds and the laughter and the company jokes would have depressed her, while the solitary time had lifted her spirits. She thought of taking the free hours she would have the next day to go shopping for something useless. Nick would be working her again soon enough. It would be fun to rummage through antique shops for a candle snuffer or pillbox.

Closing her eyes, she stretched luxuriously. Maybe this was the time to steal a couple of days and drive up to see Lindsay and Seth. She frowned when Nick's image flew into her mind.

His quiet, gentle kiss had cracked the very foundations of her defense against him. For days she hadn't allowed herself to think of him in anything but professional terms. He was the main reason, she was finally forced to admit, that she hadn't been able to face the cast party.

She wanted him. No matter how many times, over the past days and weeks, she had refused to accept that thought, her desire simply hadn't changed. But yes, it had—she wanted him more. The longing was difficult enough, but when hints of something else, something more complicated, intruded, Ruth tightly closed the door on it.

"I'm too tired to think about that now," she told a totally disinterested Nijinsky. "I'm going to bed." When he made no sign of acknowledgment, Ruth rose and stepped over him to switch off the television.

Leaving the plate of cookie crumbs for morning, she flicked off all the lights on her way to bed.

Nick stared up at the dark windows of Ruth's apartment. It's one o'clock in the morning, and she's asleep. If I had any brains, I'd be asleep, too, he said fiercely to himself.

He jammed his hands into his pockets and started to walk. You've no business here, Davidov, he told himself. You've known that all along. The night was cooling with the first true hint of fall. He hunched his shoulders against it. He'd been an idiot to come. He had told himself that over and over as he had steadily walked the blocks to her apartment building.

If she had been at the party, if he could just have looked at her... Oh, God, he thought desperately, he was long past the time when looking was enough. The nights were driving him mad, and no other woman would do. He needed Ruth.

How long had it been going on? he demanded of himself, never giving a glance as a police car sped by, sirens screaming. A month, a year? Five years? Since that moment in Lindsay's studio when he had first watched Ruth at the barre? He should have known, with that first impossible stir of desire. Good Lord, she'd only been seventeen!

How was he to have known she would taste that way when he kissed her? Or that she would respond as if she had only been sleeping—waiting for him? How was he to have known that the sight of that small, slim body would torment him day after day, night after night? Even when he danced with her, the thought of taking her, of having her melt against him, throbbed through him until he knew he would go mad. He began to walk away.

Nick stopped and turned around. Good God, he wanted her. Now. Tonight.

The banging at her door had Ruth sitting straight up in bed. What was the dream she had been having? *Nick?* She shook her head to clear it. Even as she reached for the clock, the banging started again. Sliding from the bed, she groped for her robe.

''I'm coming!'' she called, urged to hurry by the ferocity of the banging. Pulling the robe on as she went, she rushed through the darkened apartment. ''For heaven's sake, you're going to wake the neighborhood!'' Ruth peered through the peephole, blinked and peered again. She fumbled for the chain; he pounded again.

They stared at each other when the door was opened. Ruth stood bewildered by the traces of temper she saw in his eyes. Her hair was a riot of confusion over the hastily drawn on robe. Her cheeks were still flushed with sleep, her eyes heavy. Nick took a step forward, knowing he had crossed over the line.

''I need you.''

Her heart skidded at the three simple words spoken quietly, roughly, as if they fought to be said. Before she knew what she was doing, Ruth held out her arms to him.

Then they were pressed together, mouth to mouth. The hunger was raw, unbelievably strong. It was a devouring kiss—long, desperate, deep. Ruth clung to the wildness of it. She felt his hand tighten its grip on her hair, pulling her head back as if in fury. His mouth left hers only to change angles and probe deeper. There was a hint of brutality, as if he would assuage all his needs by a single kiss.

"I want you." It was a groan from a well within him as he drew her away. His eyes were dark and burning. "God, too much."

Ruth gripped the front of his sweater until her fingers hurt. "Not too much," she whispered. She drew him inside.

Her throat was dry with the pounding of her heart as she closed the door and turned to him. They were only silhouettes as they stood, inches apart, in the dark.

She swallowed, sensing his struggle for control. It wasn't control she wanted from him. Not tonight. She wanted him to be driven—for her, by her. The overwhelming need to have him touch her was terrifying. Slowly, hardly conscious of her actions, Ruth reached up to draw the robe from her shoulders. She let it slide soundlessly to the floor as it left her naked.

"Love me," she murmured.

She heard his low groan of surrender as he drew her into his arms. His mouth was hot, his hands rough and possessive. She could feel the urgency of his need.

Ruth tugged at his sweater as they moved toward the bedroom. Somewhere in the hallway she pulled it over his head and threw it to the floor. His muscles flowed under her hands.

They were at the bedroom door when she fumbled with the snap of his jeans. She felt his stomach suck in as her fingers glided over it and heard his hoarse, muffled Russian as his teeth nipped into her shoulder. His hips were narrow, the skin warm. He dug his fingers into her back when she touched him.

"Milenkaya," he said and managed a rough laugh. "Let me get my shoes off."

"I can't." The need was overpowering. She'd already waited so long. "Lie with me." She pulled him toward the bed. "Take me now, Nick. I'll go mad if you don't."

Then they were naked, and he was on top of her. Ruth could hear his heart's desperate race, his ragged breath against her ear. He was trembling, she realized, as he entered her. Her body took over, knowing its own needs, while her mind shuddered with the onslaught of sensations. One moment she was strong, the next weak and spent. Nick lay atop her, his face buried in her hair.

"Sweet God, Ruth." He heaved out the words on labored breaths. "Untouched. Untouched and I take you like a beast!" Nick rolled from her, running a hand through his hair. When he sat up, Ruth could see just the outline of his chest and shoulders, the glimmer of his eyes. "I should have known better. There's no excuse for it. I must have hurt you."

"No." She felt drugged and dizzy, but there was no pain. "No."

"It should never have been like this."

"Are you saying you're sorry this happened?"

"Yes, by God!"

The answer hurt, but she sat up and spoke calmly. "Why?"

"It's obvious, isn't it?" He rose. "I come to your door in the middle of the night and push you into bed without the smallest show of..." He groped for a word, struggling for the English equivalent of his meaning.

"Pushed me into bed?" Ruth repeated. "And of course, I had nothing to do with it." She kneeled on the bed and tossed back her hair. Nick saw the glimmer of her angry eyes. "You conceited ass! Who pushed whom into bed? Let's just get the facts straight, Davidov. *I* opened the door, *I* told you what I wanted, *I* took your clothes off. So don't act like this was all your idea. If you want to be sorry you made love to me, go right ahead." She continued to storm before he could open his mouth to speak. "But don't hide behind guilt just because I was a virgin. I was a virgin because I wanted to be. I chose the time to change it. *I* seduced *you!*" she finished furiously.

"Well." Nick spoke again after a long moment of silence. "It seems I've been put in my place."

Ruth gave a short laugh. She was angry and hurt and still throbbing. "That'll be the day."

Nick walked back to the bed and touched her hair with his hand. There were times he thought it would be easier to speak in Russian. His feelings were more clearly articulated in his native tongue.

"Ruth, it is sometimes, when I am upset, difficult to make myself understood." He paused a moment, working out the way to make himself clear. "I'm not sorry to have made love with you. This is something I've wanted for a very long time. I am sorry that your first experience in love had to be so lacking in romance. Do you see?" He cupped her face in his hands and lifted it. "This was not the way to show an innocent the delights of what a man and woman can have."

Ruth looked at him. She could see more clearly now as her eyes grew accustomed to the dark. His face was vital and alive. She felt the warmth flowing back. She smiled.

"There's another way?" she asked, keeping the smile from her voice.

His fingers traced her cheekbones. "Many other ways."

"Then I think you owe it to me to show me." She slipped her arms around his neck. "Now."

"Ruth—"

"Now," she repeated before she pressed her mouth to his. With a groan, Nick let her taste fill him again. He lingered over the kiss, exciting her with his lips and teeth and tongue. Ruth felt her blood begin to swim.

Gently, so that his thumbs just brushed her nipples, he cupped her breasts. They were small and firm and smooth. The points were taut, and he stroked easily until he heard her breath quicken. Taking his mouth to her ear, he whispered words that meant nothing to her. But the sound of them, the flutter of warm breath, dissolved her. He slid his hands to her back, supporting her as she kneeled on the bed. Already she was trembling, but he used only his lips to entice—waiting, waiting.

Slowly, with infinite care, he began to stroke her until her skin was hot against him. He seemed to find the skin on the inside of her thighs irresistible. Again and again he returned there with teasing touches. Once he caressed the triangle between her legs, and her body shuddered as she pressed against his hand. But he retreated to mold her hips and take her deep with a kiss.

The sound of her own breathing was shouting in her ears. As he pressed her back on the bed, she moaned his name.

"There's more, *milaya,*" he murmured, feasting on the flavor of her throat. "Much more."

Her breath caught in a gasp and a moan all at once as he took her nipple between his teeth. His tongue became moist as he suckled. Ruth pressed him closer, unaware of the seductive rhythm her body set under his. He took his mouth to her other breast, and shock coursed through her. She called for him mindlessly, steeped in sensation.

His mouth roamed lower and lower as his hands reached for her breasts, still hot and moist from his mouth. He guided her, as he had once guided her to music, setting the pace for their private *pas de deux*. Again he was the composer, she the dancer, moving to his imagination. Her mind was swept clean. She was utterly his.

She opened for him, and as he entered her, his mouth came greedily down on hers. He moved inside her slowly, ignoring the desperate pressure in his loins for his own release. He took her as though he had a lifetime to savor the ultimate pleasure.

Seconds, minutes, hours, they were joined until both were wild with need. With his mouth still fastened on hers, Nick took them both to the climax.

Drained, aching, Ruth lay tight against him, her head nestled on his chest. He stroked her hair now and then, winding the ends around his fingers. Under her ear Ruth could hear the deep, steady rhythm of his heart. There was no light through the windows. The room was dark and warm and silent.

This, she thought languidly, this is what I've been waiting for. This is the end of my privacy. He knows all my secrets now. Tonight I've given him everything I've ever held inside me. She sighed. "You won't go," she murmured, closing her eyes. "You won't go tonight?"

There was quiet for a moment, their own personal silence. "No," he said softly. "I won't go."

Content, Ruth curled against him and slept.

Chapter Nine

Nijinsky leaped onto the bed, wanting his breakfast. He stared, slant-eyed, at Nick for a moment, then calmly padded over his legs and stomach to stand on his chest. Feeling the pressure, Nick stirred and opened his eyes to look straight into the cat's. They regarded each other in silence. Nick brought his hands up and obligingly scratched Nijinsky's ears.

"Well, *priyatel,* you seem to have no objection in finding me here?"

Nijinsky arched his back and stretched, then settled his full length on Nick's chest. Still absently scratching the cat's ears, Nick turned his head to look at Ruth.

She was curled tightly to his side. Indeed, his arm held her firmly there. Her hair looked thick and luxurious spread over the pillowcase. Her breathing was even and deep, her lips slightly parted. She looked impossibly young—too young to feel that wild desire she had shown him. She looked like the sleeping princess, but Nick knew she was more Carlotta than Aurora. She was more fire than flower. He bent down to kiss her.

Ruth awoke to passion, her body tingling into arousal. She sighed and reached for him as his hands began a sure, steady quest. Nijinsky, caught between them, made his disapproval vocal.

Ruth gave a throaty laugh as Nick swore. "He wants his breakfast," she explained. Her eyes were still sleepy as she smiled up at Nick. Experimentally, she lifted her hand to rub his chin with her palm. "I've always wanted to do that," she told him. "Feel a man's beard the first thing in the morning."

Nick slid his hand down to fondle her breast. "I prefer softer things. Your mouth," he specified, lowering his head to nibble at it. "Very soft, very warm."

Nijinsky padded forward to butt his head between theirs. Nick narrowed his eyes at the cat. "My affection for this creature," he stated mildly, "is rapidly fading."

"He likes to keep on schedule," Ruth explained. "He always wakes me right before the alarm goes off." On cue, the clock set off a low, monotonous buzz. "See?" She laughed as Nick reached over her and slammed the button in. "What first?" she asked him "Shower or coffee?"

He leaned over her still, and his smile was slow. "I had something else in mind."

"Class," she reminded him and slipped quickly from the bed.

Nick watched her walk naked to the closet and pull out a robe. She was slim as a wand, with long legs and no hips—a boyish figure, had it not been for the pure femininity of her gait. As she reached inside the closet, he saw the small thrust of her breast under her outstretched arm. The robe passed over her, and she crossed it in front and belted it. She turned and smiled.

"Well?" she said, flipping her long hair out of the collar of the robe. "Do you want coffee?"

"You are exquisite," he murmured.

Ruth's hands faltered at the knot of the belt. She wondered if she would ever grow used to that tone of voice or that look in his eyes. She knew what would happen if she walked back to the bed. Her body began to tingle, as if his hands were already roaming it. Nijinsky growled.

"Since I'm the first up," she said, casting the cat a rueful glance, "I'll have the shower first." She arched her brows at Nick. "You can make the coffee." As she darted into the bath, she called over her shoulder, "Don't forget to feed the cat."

Ruth turned on the shower and stripped. Should it feel so right? she asked herself as she bundled her hair on top of her head. When I woke next to him, should I have felt that he simply belonged there? She had experienced no shyness, none of the awkwardness that she had been certain would have come after her first time. Ruth stepped under the shower and let the water hit her hot and strong.

But I knew it would be him. Somehow I always knew. Shaking her head, she reached for the soap. I must be crazy. How could I know it would be like this? She soaped herself and let her mind drift. They had had meals together between classes and rehearsals. They had been at the same parties. But there had never been any planned, conventional dates between them.

Should there have been? she wondered. Certainly last night had been no ordinary consummation of a typical relationship. Nick had seen her sweat and swear and rage, seen her weep. His hands had worked pain from her calves and feet. But she knew him only as well as he allowed himself to be known.

Ruth shut off the water. It was too soon, she decided, to explore her heart too deeply. She understood pain, had lived with it, but wouldn't deliberately seek it out. Nick could bring her pain. That, too, she had always known.

After toweling briskly, she slipped back into her robe and walked into the bedroom. She could hear Nick talking to Nijinsky in the kitchen. She smiled and began to pull leotards and tights from her drawer. There was something essentially right about Nick's voice carrying to her through the small apartment. She knew the cat would be much too busy attacking his breakfast to enjoy the conversation, but it pleased her. Another small bond. How many mornings had she held conversations with the disinterested cat?

Nick came into the bedroom with two steaming mugs in his hands. He was naked. His body was glorious; lean and muscled from the rigors of his profession. He strode into the room without the slightest hint of self-consciousness. Another man, Ruth mused, would have pulled on his jeans. Not Davidov.

"It's hot," he stated, setting both mugs down on the dresser before pulling Ruth into his arms. "You smell so good," he murmured against her neck. "The scent of you follows me everywhere."

His chin was raspy against her skin. She laughed, enjoying it.

"I must shave, yes?"

"Yes," Ruth agreed before she turned her mouth into the kiss. "It would hardly do for Davidov to come to class unshaven." They kissed again. His hands went to her hips to bring her closer.

"You have a razor?" He took his mouth to her ear.

"Hmmm. Yes, in the medicine cabinet." Ruth let her fingers trail up his spine. She gave a muffled shriek when he bit her earlobe.

"The shaving will wait," he decided, drawing her away to pick up his coffee. He sipped and then rose.

"Will you have to go to your apartment for clothes?" Ruth watched the easy rhythm of his muscles before he disappeared into the bath.

"I have things at my office." She heard the shower spurt back to life. "And a fresh razor."

He sang in Russian in the shower. Music was an intrinsic part of him. She found herself humming along as she went into the bath to brush her teeth. "What does it mean?" she asked with a mouthful of toothpaste.

"It's old," he told her. "And tragic. The best Russian songs are old and tragic."

"I was in Moscow once with my parents." Ruth rinsed her mouth. "It was beautiful . . . the buildings, the snow. You must miss it sometimes."

Ruth didn't have time to scream when he grabbed her and pulled her into the shower with him.

"Nick!" Blinded by streaming water, she pushed at her eyes. Her clothes were plastered against her. "Are you crazy?"

"I needed you to wash my back," he explained, drawing her closer. "But now I think there is a better idea."

"Wash your back!" Ruth struggled against him. "You might notice, I'm fully dressed."

"Oh, yes?" He smiled affably. "That's all right, I'll fix that." He pulled the soaked leotard over her shoulders so that her arms were effectively pinned.

"I've already had my shower." Ruth laughed, exasperated, and continued to struggle.

"Now you can have mine. I'm a generous man."

He fastened his mouth on hers as the water poured over them.

"Nick." His hands were wandering, loosening clothes as they went. "We have class." But she had stopped struggling.

"There's time," he murmured, sighing deeply as he found her breast. "We make time."

He drew the tights down over her hips.

Arabesque, pirouette, arabesque, pirouette. Ruth turned and lifted and bent to the commands. The practice was rigorous, as always. Her body, like the bodies of the other students, was drenched with sweat. Every day, seven days a week, they went over and over the basic steps. Professionals. Class was as much a part of a professional dancer's life as shoes and tights.

The small, intimate details were drummed into their minds at the earliest age. Who noticed the two little steps before a *jeté?* Only a dancer.

Muscles must be constantly tuned. The body must be constantly made to accept the unnatural lines of the dance. *Fifth position. Plié.* Even a day's respite would cause the body to revolt. *Port de bras.* The arms and hands must know what to do. A wrong gesture could destroy the line, shatter a mood. *Attitude.* Hold it— one, two, three, four. . . .

"Thank you."

Company class was over. Ruth went for her towel to mop her face. A shower, she thought, wiping the sweat from her neck.

"Ruth."

She glanced up at Nick. He, too, was wet. His hair curled damply around his sweatband.

"Meet me downstairs. Five minutes."

"Five minutes?" Alerted, she slung the towel over her shoulders. "Is something wrong?"

"Wrong?" He smiled, then bent and kissed her, oblivious to the other members of the company. "What should be wrong?"

"Well, nothing." A bit confused, she frowned up at him. "Why, then?"

"You have nothing scheduled for today." It was a statement, not a question, but she still shook her head. "I've seen that I don't, either." He leaned close. "We're going to play."

A smile began to tug at her mouth. "Play?"

"New York is a very entertaining city, yes?"

"So I've heard."

"Five minutes," he repeated and turned away.

Ruth narrowed her eyes at his back. "Fifteen."

"Ten," Nick countered without stopping.

Ruth dove for her bag and dashed for the showers.

In somewhere under ten minutes Ruth came downstairs, freshly washed, clad in jeans and a loose mauve sweater. Her hair was as free as her mood. Nick was already waiting, impatient, parrying questions from two male soloists.

"I'll speak to him tomorrow," he said, moving away from them when he spotted Ruth. "You're late," he accused, propelling her toward the door.

"Nope. On the minute."

They pushed through the door together.

The noise level was staggering. Somewhere to the left a road crew was tearing up the sidewalk, and the jackhammer shot its machine-gunning sound through the air. Two cabs screeched to a halt in front of them, nose to nose. Their drivers rolled down the windows and swore enthusiastically. Pedestrians streamed by without notice or interest. From a window across the street poured the hot, harsh sounds of punk rock.

"An entertaining city, yes?" Nick slipped his hand through Ruth's arm to clasp hers. Looking down, he gave her a quick grin. "Today, it's ours."

Ruth was suddenly breathless. None of their years together, none of the wild, searing love-making, had had the impact of that one intimate, breezy look.

"Where—where are we going?" she managed, struggling to come to terms with what was happening to her.

"Anywhere," Nick told her and pulled her to him for a hard kiss. "Choose." He held her tight a moment, and Ruth found she was laughing.

"That way!" she decided, throwing her hand out to the right.

Summer had vanished overnight. The cooler air made the walking easy, and they walked, Ruth was sure, for miles. They investigated art galleries and bookstores, poking here, prodding there and buying nothing. They sat on the edge of a fountain and watched the crowds passing while they drank hot tea laced with honey.

In Central Park they watched sweating joggers and tossed crumbs to pigeons. There was a world to observe.

In Saks, Ruth modeled a glorious succession of furs while Nick sat, fingers steepled together, and watched.

"No," he said, shaking his head as Ruth posed in a hip-length blue fox, "it's no good."

"No good?" She rubbed her chin against the luxurious collar with an unconscious expression of sensual pleasure. "I like it."

"Not the fur," Nick corrected. "You." He laughed as Ruth haughtily raised her brows. "What model walks with her feet turned out like that?"

Ruth looked down at her feet, then grinned. "I suppose I'm more at home in leotards than furs." She did a quick *pirouette* that had the sales clerk eyeing her warily. "And it would be hot in class." She slipped it off, letting the satin lining linger over her skin.

"Shall I buy it for you?"

She started to laugh, then saw that he was perfectly serious. "Don't be silly."

"Silly?" Nick rose as Ruth handed the clerk the fur. "Why is this silly? Don't you like presents, little one?"

She knew he used the term to goad her, but she only gave him a dry look. "I live for them," she said throatily, for the clerk's benefit. "But how can I accept it when we've only just met?" With a smoldering glance, she caressed his cheek. "What would you tell your wife?"

"There are some things wives need not know." His voice was suddenly thickly Russian. "In my country, women know their place."

"Mmm." Ruth slipped her arm through his. "Then perhaps you'll show me mine."

"A pleasure." Nick gave the wide-eyed clerk a wolfish grin. "Good day, madam." He swept Ruth away in perfect Cossack style.

"Such wickedness," he murmured as they walked from the store.

"I just love it when you're Russian, Nikolai."

He cocked an eyebrow. "I'm always Russian."

"Sometimes more than others. You can be more American than a Nebraska farmer when you want to be."

"Is this so?" He looked intensely interested for a moment. "I hadn't thought about it."

"That's why you're so fascinating," Ruth told him. "You don't think about it, you just are." Her hand linked with his as they walked. "I've wondered, Do you think in Russian and then have to translate yourself?"

"I think in Russian when I am..." He searched for the word. "Emotional."

"That covers a lot of ground." She grinned up at him. "You're often emotional."

"I'm an artist," he returned with a shrug. "We are entitled. When I'm angry, Russian is easier, and Russian curses have more muscle than American."

"I've often wondered what you were saying when you're in a rage." She gave him a hopeful glance, and he laughed, shaking his head. "You spoke to me in Russian last night."

"Did I?" The look he gave her had Ruth's heart in her throat. "Perhaps you could say I was emotional."

"It didn't sound like cursing," she murmured.

His hand was suddenly at the back of her neck, drawing her near. "Shall I translate for you?"

"Not now." Ruth calculated the distance between Fifth Avenue and her apartment. Too far, she thought. "Let's take a bus." She laughed, her eyes on his.

Nick grinned. "A cab," he countered and hailed one.

Sunlight flooded the bedroom. They hadn't taken the time to draw the blinds. They lay tangled together, naked and quiet after a storm of love-making. Content, Ruth drifted between sleep and wakefulness. Beneath her hand, Nick's chest rose and fell steadily; she knew he slept.

Forever, she thought dreamily. I could stay like this forever. She cuddled closer, unconsciously stroking his calf with the bottom of her foot.

"Dancer's feet," he murmured, and she realized that the small movement had awakened him. "Strong and ugly."

"Thanks a lot." She nipped his shoulder.

"A compliment," he countered, then shifted to look down at her. His eyes were sleepy, half-closed. "Great dancers have ugly feet."

She smiled at his logic. "Is that what attracted you to me?"

"No, it was the back of your knees."

Ruth laughed and turned her face into his neck. "Was it really? What about them?"

"When I dance with you, your arms are soft, and I wonder how the back of your knees would feel." Nick leaned up on his elbow to look at her. "How often have I held your legs—for a lift, to ease a cramp? But always there are tights. And what, I say to myself, would it be like to touch?"

Sitting up, he took her calf in his hand. "Here." His fingers slid up to the back of her knees. "And here." He saw her eyes darken, felt the pulse quicken where his fingers pressed. "So, I am nearly mad from wondering if the softness is everywhere. Soft voice, soft eyes, soft hair."

His voice was low now and quiet. "And I hold your waist to balance you, but there are leotards and costumes. What is the skin like there?" He trailed his hand up over her thigh and stomach to linger at her waist. His fingers followed the contours of her ribcage to reach her breast.

"Small breasts," he murmured, watching her face. "I've felt them pressed against me, seen them lift and fall with your breathing. How would they feel in my hand? What taste would I find there?" He lowered his mouth to let his tongue move lightly over her.

Ruth's limbs felt weighted, as though she had taken some heady drug. She lay still while his hands and mouth explored her, while his voice poured over her. He moved with aching slowness, touching, arousing, murmuring.

"Even on stage, with the lights and the music everywhere, I thought of touching you. Here." His fingers glided over her inner thigh. "And tasting. Here." His mouth moved to follow them. "You would look at me. Such big eyes, like an owl. I could almost see your thoughts and wondered if you could see mine." He pressed his lips against the firm muscles of her stomach and felt her quiver of response. "And what would you do *milaya,* if you knew how I was aching for you?"

His tongue glided over her navel. She moaned and moved under him. She had never experienced pleasure such as this—a thick, heavy pleasure that made her body hum, that weighted on her mind until even thoughts were sensations.

"So long," he murmured. "Too long, the wanting went on. The wondering."

His hands, though still gentle, became more insistent. They broke through the dark languor that held her. Her body was suddenly fiercely alive. She was acutely aware of her surroundings: the texture of the sheet against her back, the tiny dust motes that spun in the brilliant sunshine, the dull throb of traffic outside the windows. There was an impossible clarity to everything around them. Then it spun into nothing but the hands and mouth which roamed her skin.

She could have been anywhere—in the snow, in the desert; Ruth felt only Nick. She heard his breathing, more labored now than it would have been after a strenuous dance. Her own melded with it. With hard, unbridled urgency, he crushed his mouth to hers. His teeth scraped her lips as they parted for him.

The kiss deepened as his hands continued to drive her nearer the edge. Ruth clutched at him, lost in delight. Then he was inside her, and she was catapulted beyond reason into ecstasy.

"*Lyubovnitsa.*" Ruth heard his voice come hoarsely from deep within him. "Look at me."

Her eyes opened heavily as she shuddered again and again with the simultaneous forces of need and delight.

"I have you," he said, barely able to speak. "And still I want you."

She crested on a mountainous peak. Nick buried his face in her hair.

Chapter Ten

Francie caught Ruth's arm as they filed in for morning class. "Where'd you disappear to yesterday?" she demanded, pulling Ruth to the barre.

"Yesterday?" Ruth couldn't prevent the smile. "Oh, I went window shopping."

Francie shot her a knowing look. "Sure. Introduce him to me sometime." Her face grew thoughtful at Ruth's quick laugh, but she hurried on. "Have you heard the news?"

Ruth executed her *pliés* as the room began to fill with other company members. Her eyes drifted to Nick, who was in a far corner with several *corps* dancers. "What news?" Look how the sun hits his hair, she thought, as if it were drawn to it.

"The television thing." Francie set herself to Ruth's rhythm so that their heads remained level. "Didn't you hear anything?"

"Leah mentioned something." Ruth sought out the blonde as she remembered the preperformance visit. "I was told nothing was definite yet."

"It is now, kiddo." Francie was gratified to see Ruth's attention come full swing back to her.

"It is?"

"Nadine worked a whale of a deal." Francie bent to adjust her leg-warmers. "Of course, she had the main man to dangle in front of their noses."

Ruth was fully aware that Francie spoke of Nick. Again her eyes traveled to him. He had his head together with Leah now. The ballerina was using her fluid hands to emphasize her words.

"What sort of deal?"

"Two hours," Francie said with relish. "Prime time. And Nick has virtually a free hand artistically. He has the name, after all, and not only in the ballet world. People who don't know a *plié* from a pirouette know Davidov. It's some kind of package deal where he agrees to do two more projects. It's him they want. Just think what this could mean to the company!"

Francie rose on her toes. "How many people can we reach in two hours on TV compared to those we reach in a whole season on stage? Oh, God, I hope I get to dance!" She lowered into a *plié*. "I'd almost be willing to go back into the *corps* for the chance. You'll do *The Red Rose*." She gave an envious sigh.

Ruth was glad it was time for class to begin.

It was difficult to concentrate. Ruth's body responded to the calls and counts while her mind dashed in a dozen directions. Why hadn't he told her?

Her hand rested on the barre as Madame Maximova put them through their paces. Ruth was aware that Nick stood directly behind her.

They had been together all day yesterday—and this morning. He had never said a word. Would she dance?

Her working leg came up and back in attitude. Will what's happened between us interfere?

As she moved out with the class for center practice, Ruth tried to think logically. It had been hardly a week since he had told her things were still unsettled. She struggled to remember what else he had said, what exactly his mood had been. He had been annoyed because her dancing had been below par—concern that she had been upset. He had been furious when she wouldn't divulge the name of the person who had leaked the information.

What had he done? Snapped his fingers and told her *that* was how much he cared for what she said. He played the tune, and she danced. It was as simple as that. Ruth frowned as she did the combination. But why did everyone seem to know things before her? One minute Nick would tell her she was the finest ballerina in the company, and the next, he didn't even bother to fill her in on what could be the most important company project of the year.

How do you figure out such a man? You don't, she reminded herself. Turning her head, she looked him straight in the eye. He's Davidov.

Nick met the look a bit quizzically, but the tempo suddenly increased from *adagio* to *allegro* and required their attention.

"Thank you," Madame Maximova said to the troupe of dripping bodies thirty minutes later. Her voice, Ruth thought fleetingly, was much more thickly Russian than Nick's, though she had been forty years in America.

"I'd like to see the entire company on stage in fifteen minutes."

Ruth lifted her eyes and caught Nick's in the glass as he made the announcement. The speculative buzzing began immediately. Dancers began to file out in excited groups. Davidov had spoken. Ruth hefted her bag over her shoulder and prepared to join them.

"One moment, Ruth." She stopped obediently at his words. Her training was too ingrained for anything else. He said something to the ballet mistress in quiet Russian which made her chuckle—a formidable achievement. With a brisk nod, she strode from the room as if her bones were a quarter of a century younger than Ruth knew them to be.

Nick crossed to Ruth, absently pulling his towel through his hands. "Your mind was not on class."

"No?"

He recognized her searching look. As usual, it disconcerted him. "Your body moved, but your eyes were very far away. Where?"

Ruth studied him for another moment as she turned over in her mind the best way to broach the subject. She settled on directness. "Why didn't you tell me about the television plans?"

Nick's brow lifted. It was a haughty gesture. "Why should I have?"

"I'm a principal dancer with the company."

"Yes." He waited a beat. "That doesn't answer my question."

"Everyone else seems to know the details." Exasperated, she flared at him. "I'm sure they're avidly discussing it in the *corps*."

"Very likely," he agreed, slinging the towel over his shoulders. "It's hardly a secret, and secrets are always avidly discussed in the *corps*."

"You might have told me yourself," she fumed, pricked by his hauteur. "I asked you about it last week."

"Last week it was not finalized."

"It was certainly finalized yesterday, and you never said a word."

She saw his lids lower—a danger signal. When he spoke, his cool tone was another. "Yesterday we were just a man and a woman." He lifted his hands to the ends of the towel, holding them lightly. "Do you think because we are lovers I should give you special treatment as a ballerina?"

"Of course not!" Ruth's eyes widened in genuine surprise at the question. The thought had simply never occurred to her. "How could you think so?"

"Ah." He gave a small nod. "I see. I'm to trust and respect your integrity, while mine is suspect."

"I never meant—" she began, but he cut her off with that imperious flick of the wrist.

"Get your shower. You've only ten minutes now." He strode away, leaving her staring and openmouthed.

When Ruth dashed into the theater, members of the company were already sitting on the wide stage or pocketed together in corners. Breathless, she settled down next to Francie.

"So." Nick spared her a brief glance. "We seem to be all here now."

He was standing stage center with his hands tucked into the pockets of dull gray sweat pants. His hair was still damp from his shower. Every eye was on him. Nadine sat in a wooden chair slightly to his right in a superbly tailored ice blue suit.

"Most of you seem to know at least the bare details of our plans to do a production for KNT-TV." His eyes swept the group, passing briefly over Ruth, then on. "But Nadine and I will now go over the finer points." He glanced at Nadine, who folded her hands and began.

"The company will do a two-hour presentation of ballet, in vignette style. It will be taped here over a two-week period beginning in one month. Naturally, we plan to include many dances from the ballets in our repertoire. Nick and I, along with Mark and Marianne," she glanced briefly at two choreographers, "have outlined a tentative program. We will, of course, work with the television director and staff on time allowances and so forth." She paused a moment for emphasis. "I needn't tell you how important this is to the company and that I expect the best from every one of you."

Nadine fell silent. Nick turned to pick up a clipboard he had left on a tree stump prop from a forest scene in *Sleeping Beauty*.

"Rehearsals begin immediately," he stated and began to read off the list of dances and roles and rehearsal halls.

It was a diversified program, Ruth concluded, trying not to hold her breath. From Tchaikovsky's *Nutcracker*—Francie gave a muffled squeal when her name was called to dance the Sugar Plum Fairy—to de Mille's *Rodeo*. Obviously, Nick wanted to show the variety and universality of ballet.

Choreographers were assigned, scenes listed. Ruth moistened her lips. Leah was Aurora and Giselle, two plum roles but fully expected. Keil Lowell was to partner Leah both as Prince Charming and as Albrecht. A young *corps* member began to weep softly as she was given her first solo.

Nick continued to read without glancing up. "Ruth, the *grand pas de deux* from *The Red Rose* and the second act *pas de deux* from *Le Corsaire*. I will partner."

Ruth let out her breath slowly and felt the tension ease from her shoulders.

"If time permits, we will also do a scene from *Carnival*."

He continued to read in his quiet, melodious voice, but Ruth heard little more. She could have wept like the young *corps* dancer. This was what she had worked for. This was the fruit of almost two decades of training. Yet even through the joy, she could feel Nick's temper lick out at her.

He doesn't understand, she thought, frustrated by his quick, volatile moods. And he's so pig-headed, I'll have to fight my way through to explain. Drawing her knees up to her chest, she studied him carefully.

Strange, she mused, for all his generosity of spirit, he doesn't give his trust easily. She frowned. *Neither do I,* she realized abruptly. We have a problem. She rested her chin on her knees. And I'm not sure yet how to solve it.

The next few weeks weren't going to be easy, personally or professionally. Personally, Ruth knew she and Nick would have to decide what they wanted from each other and what each could give. She tucked the problem away, a little awed by it.

Professionally, it would be a grueling time. Nick as a choreographer or director was difficult enough, but as a partner, he was the devil himself. He accepted no less than perfection and had never been gentle about showing his displeasure with anything short of it. Still, Ruth would have walked over hot coals to dance with him.

Rehearsals would be exhausting for everyone. The time was short, the expectations high, and a good portion of the company were performing *Sleeping Beauty* every night for the next two weeks. Tempers and muscles would be strained. They would be limping home at night to soak their feet in ice or hot baths. They would pull each other's toes and rub each other's calves and live on coffee and nerves. But they would triumph; they were dancers.

Ruth rose with the others when Nick finished. Seeing he was already involved with Nadine, she went to the small rehearsal hall he had assigned to her. She left the door open. Company members streamed down the corridor. There was talk and raised voices. Already the sound of music flowed out from another room down the hall. Stravinsky.

Ruth walked to a bench to change to her toe shoes. She looked at them absently. They would last two or three more days, she decided. They were barely a week old. Idly, she wondered how many pairs she had been through already that year. And how many yards of satin? She crossed the ribbon over her ankle and looked up as Nick walked into the room. He closed the door behind him, and they were cut off from music and voices.

"We do *Le Corsaire* first," he stated, crossing the room to sit on the bench. "We work without an accompanist for now. They are at a premium, and I have still to block it out." He pulled down his sweat pants so that he wore only tights and the unitard.

"Nick, I'd like to talk to you."

"You have a complaint?" He slipped leg-warmers over his ankles.

"No. Nick—"

"Then you are satisfied with your assignment? We begin." He rose, and Ruth stood to face him.

"Don't pull your *premier danseur* pose on me," she said dangerously.

He lifted his brow, studying her with cool blue eyes. "I am *premier danseur*."

"You're also a human being, but that isn't the point." She could feel the temper she had ordered herself to restrain running away with her.

"And what," he said in a tone entirely too mild, "is the point?"

"What I said this morning had nothing to do with the casting." She put her hands on her hips, prepared to plow her way through the wall he had thrown up between them.

"No? Then perhaps you will tell me what it had to do with. I have a great deal to do."

Her eyes kindled. Her temper snapped. "Go do it then. I'll rehearse alone." She turned away, only to be spun back around.

"I say when and with whom you rehearse." His eyes were as hot as hers. "Now say what you will say so we can work."

"All right, then." Ruth jerked her arm from his hold. "I didn't like being kept in the dark about this. I think I should have heard it from you, straight out. Our being lovers has nothing to do with it. We're dance partners, professional partners. If you can tell half the company, why not me?" She barely paused for breath. "I didn't like the way I had to get tidbits, first from Leah, and then—"

"So, it was Leah." Nick interrupted her tirade with quiet words. Ruth let out a frustrated breath. Temper had betrayed her into telling him what she had promised herself she never would.

"It doesn't matter," she began, but the flick of his wrist stopped her again.

"Don't be stupid," he said impatiently. "There is no excuse for a dancer deliberately disturbing another before a performance. You won't tell me it was not intentional?'' He waited, watching her face. Ruth opened her mouth, and closed it again. She didn't lie well, even in the best of circumstances. "So don't pretend it doesn't matter," Nick concluded.

"All right," she conceded. "But it's done. There's no use stirring up trouble now."

Nick was thoughtful a moment. Ruth saw that his eyes were hard and distant. She knew very well he was capable of handing out punishment without compassion. "No," he said at length, "I have a need for her at the moment. We have no one who does Aurora so well, but..." His words trailed off, and Ruth knew his mind was fast at work. He would find a way of disciplining Leah and keeping his Aurora dancing. A whip in a velvet glove, Ruth thought ruefully. That was Davidov.

"In any case," she continued, bringing his attention back to her, "Leah isn't the point, either."

Nick focused on her again. "No." He nodded, agreeing to this. "You were telling me what was."

Calmer now, Ruth took a moment to curb her tongue. "I was upset when I heard this morning that things had been arranged. I suppose I felt shut out. We hadn't talked reasonably about dancing since the night we rehearsed together for *The Red Rose*. I was angry then."

"I wanted you," he said simply. "It was difficult."

"For both of us." Ruth took a deep breath. "I had never considered you would treat me differently professionally because we've become lovers. I couldn't stand to think you would. But I was nervous about the casting. I always am."

"That was perhaps an unwise thing for me to say."

Ruth smiled. Such an admission from Davidov was closer to an apology than she had hoped for.

"Perhaps," she agreed with her tongue in her cheek.

His brow lifted. "You still have trouble with respect for your elders."

"How's this?" she asked and stuck out her tongue.

"Tempting." Nick pulled her into his arms and kissed her, long and hard. "Now, I will tell you once so that it is understood." He drew her away again but kept his hands on her shoulders. "I chose you for my partner because I chose to dance with the best. If you were less of a dancer, I would dance with someone else. But it would still be you I wanted at night."

A weight was lifted from her shoulders. She was satisfied that Davidov wanted her for herself and danced with her because he respected her talent.

"Only at night?" she murmured, stepping closer.

Nick gave her shoulders a caress. "We will have little else but the night for ourselves for some time." He kissed her again, briefly, roughly, proprietarily. "Now we dance."

They went to the center of the room, faced the mirrors and began.

Chapter Eleven

Days passed; long, exhausting days filled with excitement and disappointments. Ruth worked with Nick as he blocked out and tightened their *pas de deux* from *Le Corsaire*. The choreography must suit the camera, he told her. If the dance was to be recorded by a lens, it had to be played to the lens. This was a different prospect all together from dancing to an audience. Even during their first improvised rehearsal Ruth realized Nick had done his homework. He worked hand in glove with the television director on angles and sequence.

Ruth's days were filled between classes and rehearsals, but her nights were often empty. Nick's duties as choreographer and artistic director kept him constantly busy. There were other rehearsals to oversee, more dances to be blocked out, budget meetings and late-night sessions with the television staff.

There was little time for the two of them at rehearsals. There they worked as dancer to dancer or dancer to choreographer, fitting movement to music. They argued, they agreed. *The Red Rose* posed little problem, though Nick altered a few details to better suit the new medium. *Le Corsaire* took most of their time. The part suited him perfectly. It was the ideal outlet for his creativity. His verve aroused Ruth's competitiveness. She worked hard.

He criticized tiny details like the spread of her fingers, praised the angle of her head and drove her harder. His vitality seemed to constantly renew itself, and it forced her to keep up or be left behind. At times she wondered how he did it: the endless dancing, the back-to-back meetings.

He had told her they would have the nights for each other, but so far that had not been the case. For the first time since she had moved into her apartment, Ruth was lonely. For as long as she could remember, she had been content with her own company. She walked to the window and opened the blinds to gaze out at the darkness. She shivered.

A knock at the door startled her, then she shook her head. No, it's not Nick, Ruth reminded herself as she crossed the room. She knew he had two meetings that night. She glanced through the peephole, then stood for several seconds with her hand on the knob. Taking a breath, she opened the door.

"Hello, Donald."

"Ruth." He smiled at her. "May I come in?"

"Of course." She stepped back to let him enter, then shut the door behind him.

He was dressed casually and impeccably in a leather jacket and twill trousers. Ruth realized suddenly that it had been weeks since they had last seen each other.

"How are you?" she asked, finding nothing else to say.

"Fine. I'm fine."

She detected a layer of awkwardness under his poise. It put her at ease. "Come, sit down. Would you like a drink?"

"Yes, I would. Scotch, if you have it." Donald moved to a chair and sat, watching Ruth pour the liquor. "Aren't you having one?"

"No." She handed him the glass before taking a seat on the sofa. "I've just had some tea." Absently, she passed her hand over Nijinsky's head.

"I heard your company's doing something for television." Donald swirled the Scotch in his glass, then drank.

"News travels fast."

"You're having some new costumes made," he commented. "Word gets around."

"I hadn't thought of that." She curled her legs under her. "Is your business going well?"

Lifting his eyes from the glass, Donald met hers. "Yes. I'm going to Paris at the end of the month."

"Really?" She gave him a friendly smile. "Will you be there long?"

"A couple of weeks. Ruth..." He hesitated, then set down his glass. "I'd like to apologize for the things I said the last time I saw you."

Her eyes met his, calm and searching. Satisfied, Ruth nodded. "All right."

Donald let out a breath. He hadn't expected such easy absolution. "I've missed seeing you. I'd hoped we could have dinner."

"No, Donald," she answered just as mildly. She watched him frown.

"Ruth, I was upset and angry. I know I said some hard things, but—"

"It isn't that, Donald."

He studied her, then let out a long breath. "I see. I should've expected there'd be someone else."

"You and I were never more than friends, Donald." There was no apology in her voice, nor anger. "I don't see why that has to change."

"Davidov?" He gave a quick laugh at her surprised expression.

"Yes, Davidov. How did you know?"

"I've eyes in my head," he said shortly. "I've seen the way he looked at you." Donald took another swallow of Scotch. "I suppose you're well-suited."

Ruth had to smile. "Is that a compliment or an insult?"

Donald shook his head and rose. "I'm not sure." For a moment he looked at her intensely. She met his gaze without faltering. "Good-bye, Ruth."

Ruth remained where she was. "Good-bye, Donald." She watched him cross the room and shut the door behind him.

After a few moments she took his half-filled glass into the kitchen. Pouring the Scotch down the sink, Ruth thought of the time they had spent together. Donald had made her happy, nothing more, nothing less. Was it true that some women were made for one man? Was she one of them?

Another knock scattered her thoughts. She caught her bottom lip between her teeth. The last thing she wanted was another showdown with Donald. Resolutely, Ruth went to the door and fixed a smile on her face.

"Nick!"

He carried two boxes, one flat, one larger, and a bottle of wine. *"Privet, milenkaya."* He stepped over the threshold and managed to kiss her over the boxes.

"But you're supposed to be in meetings tonight." Ruth closed the door as he dropped the boxes on her dinette table.

"I cancelled them." He gave her a grin and pulled her against him. "I told you artists are entitled to be temperamental." He made up for his brief first kiss with a lingering one. "You have plans for tonight?" he murmured against her ear.

"Well..." Ruth let the word hang. "I suppose I could alter them—with the right incentive." It felt so good to be held by him, to feel his lips on her skin. "What's in the boxes?"

"Mmmm. This and that." Nick drew her away. "That is for later," he said, pointing to the large box. "This is for now." With a flourish he tossed open the lid of the flat one.

"Pizza!"

Nick leaned over, breathing in its aroma with closed eyes. "It is to die over! Go, get plates before it's cold."

Ruth turned to obey.

"I'll sweat it off you in rehearsal tomorrow." He picked up the wine. "I need a corkscrew."

"What's in the other box?" Ruth called out as she clattered the dishes.

"Later. I'm hungry." When she came back, hands filled with plates and glasses, he was still holding the wine while stooping over to greet Nijinsky. "You'll have your share." Watching him, Ruth felt her heart expand.

"I'm so glad you're here."

Nick straightened and smiled. "Why?" He took the corkscrew from her fingers.

"I love pizza," Ruth told him blandly.

"So, I win your heart through your stomach, yes? It's an old Russian custom." The cork came out with a muffled pop.

"Absolutely." Ruth began busily to transfer pizza from box to plates.

"Then you'll bounce on stage like a little round meatball." Nick sat across from her and poured the wine. "It seems time permits for *Carnival* as well. You do Columbine."

"Oh, Nick!" Ruth, her mouth full of pizza, struggled to swallow and say more.

"The extra rehearsals will help to keep you from getting chubby."

"Chubby!"

"I don't want to strain my back in the lifts." He gave her a wicked smile.

"And what about you?" she asked sweetly. "Who wants to watch Harlequin with a paunch?"

"My metabolism," he told her smugly, "would never permit it." He wolfed down the pizza and reached for his wine. "I've been watching movies," he told her suddenly. "Fred Astaire, Gene Kelly. Such movement. With the right camera work we see all a dancer is. Angles are the key."

"Did you see *An American in Paris?*" Ruth finished off her slice and reached for the wine. "I'd love to do a time step."

"A new set of muscles," Nick mused, looking through her. "It would be interesting."

"What are you thinking?"

His eyes came back to hers and focused. "A new ballet with some of your typically American moves. It's for later." He shook his head as if filing the idea away. "So, have some more." He slid another piece onto Ruth's plate. "When one sins, one should sin magnificently."

"Another old Russian custom?" Ruth asked with a grin.

"But of course." He poured more wine into her glass.

They finished the pizza, giving the cat a whole piece for himself. Nick filled her in on the progress of rehearsals, dropping little bits of company gossip here and there to amuse her. When he began to question her about dance sequences in movies he hadn't seen, Ruth did her best to describe them.

"Are you thinking of writing this new ballet with television in mind?" she asked as they cleared the dishes. "For one of the other two projects you've agreed to do?"

"Perhaps." He was vague. "Nadine would like also a documentary on the company. It's being considered. I learned some when they taped *Ariel* and other ballets, but the cameras were always apart. Ah..." He groped for the word closer to his meaning. "Remote?" Satisfied, he continued. "This time they'll be everywhere, and this director has more knowledge of the dance than others I've worked with. It makes a difference," he concluded and smiled as Ruth handed him a dish to dry. "I've missed you."

Ruth looked up at him. They had been together for hours every day, but she knew what he meant. There was something steadying about standing together in the kitchen. "I've missed you, too."

"We can make a little time when this is over, before new rehearsals begin. A few days." Nick set down the dish and touched her hair. "Will you come with me to California?"

His house in Malibu, she thought and smiled. "Yes." Forgetting the dishes, she slipped her arms around his waist and held him. They were silent for a moment, then Nick bent and kissed the top of her head.

"Don't you want to know what's in the other box?"

Ruth groaned. "I can't eat another thing."

"More wine?" he murmured, moving his lips down her temple.

"No." She sighed. "Just you."

"Come, then." Nick drew her away, then offered his hand. "It's been too long."

They walked from the kitchen, but Ruth's eyes fell on the unopened box. "What *is* in there?"

"I thought you weren't interested."

Unable to restrain her curiosity, Ruth lifted the lid. She stared and made no sound.

There, where she had expected some elaborate pastries or a huge cake, was the soft, thick pelt of the blue fox she had modeled in Saks. Touching it with her fingertips, she looked up at Nick.

"It's not fattening," he told her.

"Nick." Ruth made a helpless gesture and shook her head.

"It suited you best. The color is good with your hair." He caught a generous handful of Ruth's hair and let it fall through his fingers. "It's soft. Like you."

"Nick." Ruth took his hands in hers. "I can't."

He lifted a brow. "I'm not allowed to give you presents?"

"Yes, I suppose." She let out a little breath. "I hadn't thought of it." He was smiling at her, making it difficult to explain logically. "But not a present like this."

"I bought you a pizza," he pointed out and brought her hand to his lips. "You didn't object."

"That's not the same thing." She made a small, exasperated sound as his lips brushed her wrist. "And you ate half of it."

"It gave me pleasure," he said simply, "as it will give me pleasure to see you in the fur."

"It's too expensive."

"Ah, I can only buy you cheap presents." He pushed up her sleeve and kissed the inside of her elbow.

Her brows lowered. "Stop making me sound fool-ish."

"You don't need my help for that." Before she could retort, he pulled her close and silenced her. "Do you find the fur ugly?" he asked.

"No, of course not. It's gorgeous." With a sigh, Ruth rested her head on his shoulder. "But you don't have to buy me anything."

"Have to? No." He ran a hand down her back to the curve of her hip. "The things I have to do, I know. This is what I choose to do." He drew her away, smiling again. "Come, try it on for me."

Ruth studied him carefully. The gesture was gener-ous, impulsive and typically Nick. How could she re-fuse? "Thank you," she said so seriously that he laughed and hugged her.

"You look at me like an owl again, very sober and wise. Now, please, let me see you wear it."

If Ruth had any doubts, the *please* brushed them aside. She was certain she could count on the fingers of one hand the times he had used the word to her personally. With no more hesitation, she dove into the box. Her fingers sank into fur.

"It is gorgeous, Nick. Really gorgeous."

"Not over your robe, *milaya*." He shook his head as Ruth started to put the coat on. "They don't wear fox with blue terry cloth."

Ruth shot him a look, then undid the knot in her belt. She slipped out of the robe and quickly into the fur. Nick felt his stomach tighten at the brief flashes of her nakedness. Her dark hair fell over the blue-toned white; her eyes shone with excitement.

"I have to see how it looks!" Ruth turned, thinking to dash to the bedroom.

"I love you."

The words stopped her dead. She felt completely winded, as though she had taken a bad fall on stage. Her breath would simply not force its way through her lungs. She closed her eyes. Her fingers were gripping the fur so tightly they hurt. She couldn't relax them. Very slowly, she turned to face him. Her throat was closing, so that when the words came, they were thick. "What did you say?"

"I love you. In English. I've told you in Russian before. *Ya tebya lyublyu.*"

Ruth remembered the words murmured in her ear—words that had jumbled in her brain when he had made love to her, when he had held her close before sleep. Her knees were beginning to shake. "I didn't know what they meant."

"Now you do."

She stared at him, feeling the trembling spread. "I'm afraid," Ruth whispered. "I've waited to hear you say that for so long, and now I'm terrified. Nick." She swallowed as her eyes filled. "I don't think my legs will move."

"Do you want to walk to me or away?"

The question steadied her. Perhaps he was afraid, too. She moved forward. When she stood in front of him, she waited until she thought her voice would be level. "How do I say it in Russian?" she asked him. "I want to say it in Russian first."

"Ya tebya lyublyu."

"Ya tebya lyublyu, Nikolai." She fumbled over the pronunciation. Ruth saw the flash of emotion in his eyes before she was crushed against him. *"Ya tebya lyublyu."* She said again, "I love you."

His mouth was on her hair, her cheeks and eyelids, then bruisingly, possessively on hers. *"Ona-moya,"* he said once, almost savagely. *"She is mine."*

The fur slipped to the floor.

Chapter Twelve

Ruth knew she had never worked so hard in her life. Performing a full-length ballet was never easy, but dancing for four cameras was very exasperating. Short sequences of step combinations had to be repeated over and over, so that she found it nearly impossible to keep the mood. She was accustomed to the lights, but the technicians' cables and the cameras intruding on the stage were another matter. She felt surrounded by them.

Her muscles cramped from the starting and stopping. Her face had to be remade up for the closeups and tight shots. The television audience wouldn't care to see beads of perspiration on an elegant ballerina. It was possible, with the distance of a stage performance, to maintain a ballerina's illusion of effortless fluidity. But the camera was merciless.

Again and again they repeated the same difficult set of *soubresauts* and pirouettes. Nick seemed inexhaustible. The camera work seemed to fascinate him. He showed no sign of annoyance with minor technical breakdowns but simply stopped, talking with the director as the television crew made ready again. Then he would repeat the steps with renewed energy.

They had been taping what would be no more than a three-minute segment for over two hours. It was an athletic piece, full of passion and spirit—the type of dance that was Nick's trademark. Again Ruth turned in a triple pirouette, felt a flash of pain and went down hard. Nick was crouched beside her in an instant.

"Just a cramp," she managed, trying to get her breath.

"Here?" Taking her calf, he felt the knotted muscle and began to work it.

Ruth nodded, though the pain was acute. She put her forehead on her knees and closed her eyes.

"Ten minutes, please," she heard Nick call out. "Did you hurt anything when you fell?" he murmured, kneading the muscle. Ruth could only shake her head. "It's a bad one," he said, frowning. "It's difficult without warmers."

"I can't do it!" She suddenly banged a fist on the stage and raised her face. "I just can't do it right!"

Nick narrowed his eyes. "What nonsense is this?"

"It's not nonsense. I can't," Ruth continued wildly. "It's impossible. Over and over, back and forth. How can I feel anything when there's no flow to it? People everywhere, practically under my nose, when I'm supposed to be preparing for a leap."

"Ignore them and dance," he said flatly. "It's necessary."

"Necessary?" she tossed back. "I'll tell you what's necessary. It's necessary to sweat. I'm not even allowed to do that. If that man dusts powder on my face once more, I'll scream." She caught her breath as a

cramp shot into her other leg. Her feet were past pain. She lowered her head again. "Oh, Nick, I'm so tired."

"So what do you do? Quit?" His voice was rough as he began to work the other leg. "I need a partner, not a complaining baby."

"I'm not a baby." Her head shot back up. "Nor a machine!"

"You're a dancer." He felt the muscle relaxing under his hand. "So dance."

Her eyes flashed at the curt tone. "Thanks for the understanding." She pushed his hand away and sprang to her feet. Her legs nearly buckled under her, but she snapped them straight.

"There's a place for understanding." He rose. "This isn't it. You've work to do. Now, go have the man with the powder fix your face."

Ruth stared at him a moment, then turned and walked offstage without a word.

When she had gone, Nick swore under his breath, then sat down again to work out the pain in his own legs.

"You're a tough man, Davidov."

Nick looked up to see Nadine rise from a chair in the audience. "Yes." He turned his attention back to his leg. "You've told me before."

"It's the way I like you." She walked to the side of the stage and climbed the steps. "But she is still young." Her heels set out an echo as she walked across the stage.

Nadine kneeled beside him. She took his leg and began to competently massage the cramp. "She's a good dancer," Nadine said casually. "Good feet, wonderful legs, very musical." She gave him a quick smile. "She's not yet as tough as we are."

"Better for her."

"More difficult for you because you love her." Nick gave her an inquiring lift of a brow. "There's nothing about my dancers I don't know," Nadine went on. "Often before they do. You've been in love with her for a long time."

"So?" Nick said.

"Dancers often pair up with dancers. They speak the same language, have the same problems." Nadine sat back on her haunches. "But when it's my *premier danseur* and artistic director involved with my best ballerina, I'm concerned."

"There's no need for it, Nadine." His tone was mild, but there was no mistaking his annoyance.

"Romances can go several ways," she commented. "Believe me, I know very well." Nadine smiled again, a bit ruefully. "Dancers are an emotional species, Nick. I don't want to lose either of you if you have a falling out. This one is destined to be *prima ballerina absolutta.*"

Nick's voice was very cool. "Are you suggesting I stop seeing Ruth?" He rose carefully to his feet. His eyes were very direct and very blue.

Nadine studied him thoughtfully. "How long have I known you, Davidov?"

He smiled briefly. "It would only age both of us, Nadine."

She nodded in agreement, then held up her hand. Nick lifted her lightly to her feet. "A long time. Long enough to know better than to suggest to you." Her look became wry. "I've watched your parade of women over the years."

"*Spasibo.*"

"That wasn't praise," she countered. "It was an observation." She paused again, briefly. "Bannion's different."

"Yes," he said simply. "Ruth's different."

"Be careful, Davidov. Falls are dangerous to dancers." She turned as technicians began to wander back toward the stage. "She'll hate you for a while."

"I'll have to deal with that."

"Of course," Nadine agreed, expecting nothing else.

Very erect, face composed, Ruth walked out of the wings. While her make-up was being repaired, she had forced everything out of her mind but the dance she was to perform. Until it was completed and on tape, she would allow herself no emotion but that which her character would feel. She crossed to Nick.

"I'm ready."

He looked down at her. He wanted to ask if there was still pain, wanted to tell her that he loved her. Instead, he said, "Good, then we start again."

Nearly two hours later Ruth stood under the shower. Her body was too numbed for pain. Her thoughts were fuzzy with fatigue. Only two things were clear: She detested dancing for the camera; and when she had needed Nick, he had stepped away. He had spoken to her as though she had been lazy and weak. That she had lost control in public had humiliated her enough. His cold words had added to it.

Her strength and stamina had always been a source of pride for her. It had been an enormous blow to have fallen to the stage, beaten and hurting. She had wanted comfort, and he had given her disdain.

Ruth stepped from the shower and wrapped herself in a towel just as Leah walked in. Still in street clothes, the blonde leaned against a sink and smiled.

"Hi." She studied Ruth's pale, exhausted face. "Rough day?"

"Rough enough." Ruth walked to her bag to pull out a sweater.

"I heard you had some trouble with your number this afternoon."

Ruth had a moment, as she pulled the sweater over her head, to compose her features. "Nothing major," she said calmly, though the easy words cost her. *"Le Corsaire's* taping is finished."

"I can't wait to see it." Leah smiled, taking out a brush and pulling it lazily through her baby fine hair. "You're looking pale," she observed as Ruth tugged on her jeans. "Lucky you have a couple of days to rest before they start taping *The Red Rose.*"

Ruth pulled up her zipper with a jerk. "You keep up with the schedules."

"I make it my business to know what's going on with everybody in the company."

Ruth sat down and took her sneakers from her bag. She put one on, then threw Leah a long, thoughtful look. "What is it you want?"

"Nick," she answered instantly. Her smile deepened as Ruth's eyes glistened. "Not that way, darling, though it's tempting." She smiled. "It appears that being his lover has its advantages."

Ruth struggled with the desire to hurl her other shoe at the smile. Seething, she slipped it on her foot. "What's between Nick and me is personal and has nothing to do with anyone." Blood pounding, Ruth got to her feet.

"Oh, but there's a connection." Leah reached out to touch Ruth's arm as she would have swung from the room.

The violent urge surprised Ruth. Her temper had never been so close to being completely, blindly lost. She let her bag drop noisily to the floor.

"What?"

Leah sat on the edge of the sink and crossed her ankles. "I intend to be *prima ballerina absolutta.*"

"Is that supposed to be news?" Ruth countered with an arched brow.

"I'm fully aware," Leah continued smoothly, "that to do that and remain with this company, I need Nick for my partner."

"Then you have a problem." Ruth faced her squarely. "Nick is my partner."

"For now," Leah agreed easily. "He'll certainly drop you when he gets tired of sleeping with you."

"That's my concern," Ruth said softly.

"Nick's lovers never last long. We've all witnessed the ebb and flow over the years. Remember the lawyer six or eight months ago? Very elegant. And there was a model before that. He usually avoids picking from the company. Very fastidious, our Nikolai."

"*My* Nikolai." Ruth picked up her bag again. "You'd better satisfy yourself with the partners you're given."

"He won't be dancing much longer than a couple more years. He's already choreographing most of the time. Two years is all I need," Leah returned flatly.

"Two years." Ruth laughed and swung the bag over her shoulder. "I'll be *prima ballerina absolutta* in six months." She let her own fury guide her words. "After the show is aired, everyone in the country will know who I am. If the competition worries you, try another company."

"Competition!" Leah's eyes narrowed. "You barely made it through your first piece." She gave Ruth one of her glittery smiles. "Nick might be persuaded to cut your other two or give them to someone with a bit more stamina."

"Such as you."

"Naturally."

"In a pig's eye," Ruth said mildly, then, shoving Leah aside, she walked out.

Though the small gesture had helped, her nerves were still stretched to the breaking point. The emotional onslaught had taken her mind off her body, and she moved down the steps oblivious to the ache in her calves. She headed for the street, seething with indignation.

"Ruth." Nick took her arm when she failed to respond the first time he called. "Where are you going?"

"Home," she said shortly.

"Fine." He studied her heated face. "I'll take you."

"I know where it is." She turned toward the door again, but his hand remained firm.

"I said I would take you."

"Very well." She shrugged. "Suit yourself."

"I usually do," he answered coolly and drew her outside and into a cab. Ruth sat in her corner with her bag held primly in her lap. Nick sat back against the seat, making no attempt at conversation. His mind was apparently occupied with his own thoughts. Stubbornness prevented Ruth from speaking.

Her scene with Nick on stage replayed in her head, followed by the scene with Leah. Ruth's anger took the form of stony silence.

When the cab pulled up in front of her apartment, she slid out her side, prepared to bid Nick a cool goodbye. He alighted from the street side, however, and rounding the rear of the cab, took her arm again. His grip was light but unarguable. Making no comment, Ruth walked with him into the building.

She knew she was primed for a fight. It would take only the smallest provocation. Anger was bubbling hot just beneath the surface. She unlocked the door to her apartment. Breezing through, she left Nick to go or come in as he chose.

From his seat on the sofa, Nijinsky rose, arched his back, then leaped soundlessly down. Dutifully, he circled around Ruth's ankles before he moved to Nick. She heard him give the cat a murmured greeting. Staying behind her wall of silence, she went into the bedroom to unpack her bag.

She lingered over the task purposefully. There was no sound from the other room as she carefully placed her toe shoes on her dresser. Meticulously, she took the pins from her hair and let it fall free. A small part of her headache fled with the lack of confinement. She brushed her hair out, letting one long stroke follow the next. The apartment remained absolutely silent.

For a full ten minutes Ruth busied herself around the bedroom, finding a dozen small, meaningless tasks that required her attention. Her nerves began to pound again. Deciding that what she needed was food, Ruth tied her hair back with a ribbon and left the room.

Nick was sound asleep on the couch. He lay on his back with a purring Nijinsky curled in a comfortable ball on his chest. His breathing was slow and even. All her resentment fled.

He's exhausted, she realized. The signs were clear on his face. Why hadn't she noticed them before? Because she had been too involved with her own feelings, she thought guiltily.

The creases were deep in his cheeks. She could see the faint mauve shadows under his eyes. Ruth sighed. She could have wept. No tears, she ordered herself firmly.

Taking a mohair Afghan from the back of a chair, she spread it up to Nick's waist. He never moved. Nijinsky opened one eye, sent her an accusing glance and settled back to sleep. Ruth sat in a chair and curled her legs under her. She watched her lover sleep.

It was dark when Nick woke. Disoriented, he pressed his fingers to his eyes. There was a weight on his chest. Moving his hand to it, he discovered a small ball of fur. He let out a long sigh as Nijinsky experimentally dug his claws in. With a halfhearted oath, Nick pushed the cat aside and sat up. A stream of light fell from the kitchen doorway. He sat for some moments longer before rising and walking to it.

Ruth stood at the stove. With her hair pulled back, Nick could study her profile: delicate bones, lifted jaw, the slight slant of her eyes. Her lips were parted in concentration—soft, generous lips he could taste just by looking. She had the slender, arching neck of a classical ballerina. He knew the precise spot where the skin was most sensitive.

She looked very young in the harsh kitchen light, much as she had looked the first time he had seen her—in the glare of sun on snow in the parking lot of Lindsay's school. Ruth turned suddenly, sensing him. Their eyes locked.

She moistened her lips. "You were stirring. I thought you'd be hungry. Are omelets all right?"

"Yes. Good."

He leaned on the door jamb as she went back to her preparation. A glance at his watch told him it was barely nine o'clock. He had slept for just under two hours. He was as refreshed as if it had been a full night.

"Can I help?"

Ruth kept her eyes on the eggs growing firm in the pan. "You could get out the plates. I'm almost done." Beside her on the counter the percolator began to pop. Nick got out plates and cups. "Do you want anything else?" she asked, hating the strained politeness of her voice.

"No. This is fine."

Expertly, Ruth flipped the first omelet from pan to plate. "Go ahead and get started. I'll just be another minute." Beaten eggs sizzled as she poured them into the pan. "I'll bring the coffee."

Nick took his plate into the dining room. Ruth continued to work, focusing all her concentration on her cooking. The percolator became more lively. She slid the eggs from the pan. Unplugging the coffee, she took it into the dining room.

Nick glanced up as she came in.

"Is it all right?" She set down her plate, then poured coffee into the waiting cups.

"It's good." He forked another mouthful. Ruth avoided his eyes and set the percolator on a trivet. Taking the seat across from him, she began to eat.

"I have to thank you for letting me sleep." Nick watched her push the eggs around on her plate. "I needed it. And this."

"You looked so tired," she murmured. "It never occurred to me that it's difficult for you."

"Ah," he said with light amusement. "Davidov the indestructible."

Ruth lifted her eyes at that. "I suppose that's how I've always seen you. How all of us see you."

His glance was steady. "But then, you are not all of us." He saw the tears spring to her eyes. Something tightened inside his stomach. "You should eat," he said briskly. "It's been a long day."

Ruth picked up her coffee cup, struggling for composure. She'd had enough scenes for one day. "I'm not really hungry."

Nick shrugged and went back to his meal. "Something's burning," he commented. With a cry, Ruth leaped up and dashed into the kitchen.

The omelet pan smoked in a steady column, its surface crackling from the heat. Swearing, she flicked off the flame she had left burning under it and gave the stove an angry kick.

"Careful," Nick said from the doorway. "I can't use a partner with broken toes."

She rounded on him, wanting to vent her anger somewhere. But he smiled. It was as though he had pulled his finger from the dam.

"Oh, Nick!" Ruth threw herself into his arms and clung. "I was so horrible today. I danced so badly."

"No," he corrected, kissing her hair. "You danced beautifully, better when you were angry with me."

Ruth drew her head back and looked at him. She knew with certainty that he would never lie about her dancing to comfort her. "I shouldn't have been angry with you. I was so wrapped up in myself, in how I was feeling, that I never thought about how difficult it was for you, too. You always make it look so easy."

"You don't like the camera."

"I hate it. It's horrible."

"But valuable."

"I know that. I know it." She drew back to stand away from him. "I hate the way I acted this afternoon, crying in front of all those people, raging at you."

"You're an artist. I've told you, it's expected."

"I don't like public displays." She took a long breath. "I particularly don't like seeing myself as selfish and uncaring."

"You're too hard on yourself, Ruth. The woman I love is not selfish and uncaring."

"I was today." She shook her head. "I didn't stop thinking of myself until I saw you sleeping, looking so utterly exhausted. I know how hard you've been working, not only on our dances but at all the other rehearsals you have to supervise and the meetings and the schedule for the rest of the season. But all I thought about was how I hated those cameras looming everywhere and about how my legs ached." She gave a quiet, shuddering sigh. "I don't like knowing I can be that one-dimensional, too much like what Donald once accused me of."

"Oh, enough." Nick took her shoulders in a firm grip. "We have to think of ourselves, of our own bodies. There's no other way to survive. You're a fool if you believe it makes you less of a person. We're different from others, yes. It's our way."

"Selfish?"

"Must it have a name?" He gave her a little shake, then pulled her against him. "Selfish, if you like. Dedicated. Obsessed. What does it matter? Does it change you? Does it change me?" Suddenly his mouth was on hers.

Ruth moaned with the kiss. His lips were both tender and possessive, sparking small flames deep inside her. He drew her closer, and still closer, until they were molded together.

"This is how I wanted to kiss you when you sat on the stage angry and hurting." His mouth moved over hers with the words. "Do you hate me because I didn't?"

"No. No, but I wanted you to." She held him tighter. "I wanted so badly for you to."

"You would never have finished the dance if I had comforted you then." Nick tilted her head back until their eyes met. "I knew that, because I know you. Does this make me cold and selfish?"

"It makes you Davidov." Ruth sighed and smiled at him. "That's all I want."

"And you are Bannion." He lowered his mouth to hers. "That's all I want."

"You make it sound so simple. Is it simple?"

"Tonight it is simple." He lifted her into his arms.

Chapter Thirteen

Ruth sat six rows back and watched the taping. Her three segments were finished. What would be perhaps nine or ten minutes of air time had taken three grueling days to tape. She had learned to play for the camera, even to tolerate it. But she knew she would never feel the excitement with it that Nick did. He had challenged her to outdo him in their *pas de deux* from *Carnival*. He had been exuberant, incredibly agile in his Harlequin mask and costume, a teasing, free-spirited soul who infused more vitality into her Columbine than she had believed possible.

He simply glows with energy, she mused, watching him on stage. Even when he's not dancing.

The *corps* was doing a scene from *Rodeo*. Amid the cowboy hats and gingham, Nick stood in a characteristically drab sweat suit and instructed the dancers. If he had worn gold or silver, he could not have been more of a focal point.

Ruth knew how little relaxation he had allowed himself over the past weeks. Yet as he coached his dancers a last time, he was as vital and alive as a young boy. How does he do it? she asked herself.

She thought of what Leah had said and wondered: Would he stop dancing in another two years? Ruth hated to think of it. He looked so young. In most professions he would be considered young, she reflected. As art director, as choreographer, as composer, he could go on indefinitely. But as *danseur noble,* time was precious.

He knew it, of course. Ruth watched as Davidov stepped out of camera range. How did he feel about it? He'd never told her. There were so many things he'd never told her.

Ruth was aware of how smoothly he changed the subject whenever she probed too deeply about his life in Russia. It wasn't a simple matter of curiosity that prompted her to ask. Yet she didn't know how to explain her questions to him.

It frustrated her that he chose to block off a part of himself from her. Privacy was something Ruth valued deeply and respected in others, but loving Nick wholeheartedly, she had the need to know him completely. Yet he continued to draw back from questions or discussions of his early life or his professional career in his own country. Nor had he spoken with her of his feelings about perhaps coming to the end of his active dancing career.

Too often, she decided, he thought of her as a little girl. How would she convince him to share his problems with her as well as his joys?

Music filled the theater; the quick, raucously Western-American music that set the mood for the dance. Nick watched the *corps* from behind a cameraman, his hands lightly balled at his hips. Ruth drew in her breath.

Will I always feel like this? she wondered. Moved by him, dazed by him? It was frightening to be in love with a legend. Even in the short time they had been together, career demands had pressured them both. Ballet was both a bond and a strain. The time they spent alone in her apartment was another world. They could be any man and woman then. But the music and the lights called them back. And here, in the world that consumed most of their lives, he was Davidov the master.

"He seems to be handling things well, as usual." Nadine slipped into the seat beside her, and Ruth snapped herself back.

The music had stopped. Nick was talking to the dancers again as the director spoke to some invisible technician on his headset. Ruth let her eyes follow Nick. "Yes, he seems to be."

"Like a boy with a new train set."

Ruth gave Nadine a quizzical look. "Train set?"

"The fresh excitement, the enthusiasm," she explained with a sweeping gesture of her hand. "He's loving this."

"Yes." Ruth looked back at Nick. "I can see that."

"Your dances went well." At Ruth's deprecating laugh, Nadine went on. "Oh, I know you had some adjustments to make. That's life."

"Were you watching?"

"I'm always watching."

"You're not usually kind, Nadine," Ruth commented wryly.

"My dear, I'm never kind. I can't afford to be." The music began again, and though Nadine's eyes were on the stage, she spoke to Ruth. "They did go well, all in all. The tape is magnificent."

"You've seen it?" Ruth was all attention now.

Nadine merely lifted her brow in response. "The program should be all we hoped for. I can say frankly that you and Nick together are the best I've seen in some time. I never thought he'd find a partner to equal Lindsay. Of course, your style and hers are very different. Lindsay took to the air as if she were part of it—effortlessly, almost mystically. You challenge it, as if defying gravity."

Ruth pondered over the description. It seemed to make perfect sense. "Lindsay was the most beautiful ballerina I've ever seen."

"We lost her because she allowed her personal life to interfere," Nadine said flatly.

"She didn't have any choice." Ruth rushed to Lindsay's defense. "When her father was killed and her mother so badly hurt, she had to go."

"We make our own choices." Nadine turned to face Ruth directly. "I don't believe in fate. We make things happen."

"Lindsay did what she had to do."

"What she chose to do," Nadine corrected. "We all do." She studied Ruth's frown. "I've had one priority all my life. I'd like to think all my dancers were the same, but I know better. You have the talent, the youth, the drive to make a very important mark in the world of ballet. Lindsay had just begun to make hers when she left. I wouldn't like to lose you.''

''Why should you?'' Ruth phrased the question carefully, keeping her eyes on Nadine. She was no longer aware of what was happening on stage.

''Temperaments run high in dancers.''

''So I've been told,'' Ruth said dryly. ''But that doesn't answer my question.''

''I need both you and Nick, Ruth, but I need Nick more.'' She paused for a moment, watching her words sink in. ''If the two of you come to a time when things are…no longer as they are, and you can't—or won't— work together, I'd have to make a choice. The company can't afford to lose Nick.''

''I see.'' Ruth turned back to the stage and stared at the dancers.

''I've thought a long time about speaking to you. I felt it best I make my position clear.''

''Have you spoken to Nick?''

''No.'' Nadine looked at Nick as he stood with the technicians. ''Not so bluntly. I will, of course, if it becomes necessary. I hope it doesn't.''

''Quite a number of dancers in the company become involved with each other,'' Ruth commented. ''Some even marry. Do you make a habit of prying into their private lives?''

''I always thought there was fire behind those scrupulous manners.'' Nadine smiled thinly. ''I'm glad to see it.'' She paused a moment. ''As long as nothing outside interferes with the company, there's no reason to create unhappiness.'' She gave Ruth another direct look. "But Nick isn't merely one of my dancers. We both know that."

"I don't think you could say that what's between Nick and me has interfered with the company or with our dancing." Ruth sat stiffly.

"Not yet, no. I'm fond of you, Ruth, which is why I spoke. Now I have to go wring a few more dollars out of a patron." Nadine rose and, without another word, moved up the dark aisle and out of the theater.

On stage, Nick watched his dancers. He saw them both individually and as a group. This one's arm wasn't arched quite right, that one's foot placement was perfect. He kept a close eye on the *corps*. There were two he planned to make soloists soon. There was a young girl, barely eighteen, whom he observed with special interest. She had an ethereal, otherworldly beauty and great speed. She reminded him a bit of Lindsay. Already he saw her as Carla in *The Nutcracker* the following year. He would have to induce Madame Maximova to work with her individually.

The director stopped the tape, and Nick moved forward to correct a few minor details. They had been working nearly two hours, and the hot lights shone without mercy.

Nadine, he thought as they began again, is like a hawk hunting chickens when she holds auditions for the *corps*. Poor children; were they ever really aware of the drudgery of dance? So few of them would ever go beyond the *corps*. Again he watched the young girl as she spun into her partner's arms. That one will, he concluded. She'll be chasing after Ruth's heels in two years.

He smiled, remembering Ruth's *corps* days. She'd been so young and very withdrawn. Only when she had danced had she been truly confident. Even then— yes, even then—he had wanted her, and it had astonished him. He had watched her grow more poised, more open. He'd watched her talent blossom.

Five years, he thought. Five years, and now, at last, I have her. Still it wasn't enough. There were nights his duties kept him late, and he was forced to go home to his own empty apartment knowing Ruth slept far away in another bed.

He wondered whether he was more impatient now because he had waited so long for her. It was a daily struggle to keep from hurrying her into a fuller commitment. He hadn't even meant to tell her he loved her, certainly not in that flat, unadorned manner. The moments before she had turned and given the love back to him had left him paralyzed with fear. Fear was a new sensation and one he discovered he didn't care for.

Part of him resented the hold she had on him. No one woman had ever occupied his thoughts so completely. And still she held part of herself aloof from him. It was tantalizing, infuriating.

He wanted her without reserves, without secrets. The longer they went on, the more impossible it became to prevent himself from pressing her for more. Even now, with his mind crammed with his work, he knew she sat out in the darkened theater. He sensed her.

She shouldn't be allowed to pull at him this way, he thought with sudden anger. Yet he wanted her there. Close. The words he had spoken when he had come to her apartment in the night grew more true as time passed. He needed her.

At last the taping session was completed. Nick spoke with the director as dancers filed offstage. They would cool their bodies under showers and nurse their aches. Ruth rose from her seat in the audience and approached the stage. The musicians were talking among themselves, stretching their backs.

"One hour, please," Nick called to them and received a grumbled response.

Technicians shut off the high wattage lights, and the temperature dropped markedly. The crew was talking about the Italian deli down the street and meatball sandwiches. With a laugh, Nick declined joining them. His offer of yogurt in his company canteen was met with unilateral disgust.

"So." He drew Ruth into his arms when she stepped onstage. "What did you think of it?"

"It was wonderful," she answered truthfully. She tried not to think about her conversation with Nadine as Nick gave her a brief kiss. "Apparently, you have a flair for Americana."

"I always thought I'd make a good cowboy." He grinned and picked up one of the abandoned prop hats. With a flourish, he set it on his head. "Now I only need six-guns."

Ruth laughed. "It suits you," she decided, adjusting the hat lower over his forehead. "Did they have cowboys in Russia?"

"Cossacks," he answered. "Not quite the same." He smiled, running his hands down her arms. "Are you hungry? There's an hour before we begin again."

"Yes."

Slipping an arm around her, he tossed off the hat as they crossed the stage. "We'll get something and take it up to my office. I want you alone."

Ten minutes later Nick closed his office door behind them. "We should have music for such an elaborate meal, yes?" He moved to the stereo.

Ruth set down their bowls of fruit salad as he switched on Rimsky-Korsakov. After turning the volume low, he came back to her.

"This first." Nick gathered her into his arms. Ruth lifted her mouth to his, hungry for his kiss.

Her demand fanned the banked fires within him. With a low sound of pleasure, he tangled his fingers in her hair and plundered. Her mouth was avid, seeking, as she let the kiss take her. Desire was a fast-driving force that rocketed inside her. She slipped her hands under his sweat shirt to feel the play of muscles on his back. His mouth began to move wildly over her face; her lips ached for his.

"Kiss me," she demanded and stopped his roaming mouth with hers.

The kiss was shattering and stormy. It was as though he poured all his needs into the single meeting of lips. It left her breathless, shaken, wanting more. He probed her lip with his teeth until she moaned in drugged excitement. Then he dove deeper, using his tongue to destroy any hold on sanity. Ruth murmured mindlessly, craving for him to touch her.

As if reading her thoughts, he brought his hand to her breast. She shuddered as the rough fabric of her cotton blouse scraped her skin. With his other hand he tugged it from the waistband of her jeans. His fingers snaked up over her ribcage and found her. Together they caught their breath at the contact.

When the phone on his desk began to ring, Nick let out a steady stream of curses. He spun to answer and yanked the receiver from the cradle.

"What is it?"

Ruth let out a long breath and sat. Her knees were trembling.

"I can't see him now." She had heard that sharp, impatient tone before and felt a small tingle of sympathy for the caller. "No, he'll wait. I'm busy, Nadine."

Ruth's brows shot up. No one spoke to Nadine that way. She sighed then and looked up at Nick. No one else was Davidov.

"Yes, I'm aware of that. In twenty minutes, then. No, twenty." He set the phone down with a final click. When he looked back down at Ruth the annoyance was still in his eyes. "It seems an open wallet requires my attention." He swore and thrust his hands into his pockets. "There are times when this business of money drives me mad. It must be forever coaxed and tugged. It was simple once just to dance. Now it's not enough. They give us little time, Ruth."

"Come and eat," she said, wanting to soothe him. "Twenty minutes is time enough."

"I don't speak of only now!" The anger rose in his voice, and she braced herself for the torrent. "I wanted to be with you last night and all the other nights I slept alone. I need more than this—more than a few moments in the day, a few nights in the week."

"Nick—" she began, but he cut her off.

"I want you to move in with me. To live with me."

Whatever she had been about to say escaped her. He stood over her, furious and demanding. "Move in with you?" she repeated dumbly.

"Yes. Today. Tonight."

Her thoughts were whirling as she stared up at him. "Into your apartment?"

"Yes." Impatient, he pulled her to her feet. "I cannot—will not—keep going home to empty rooms." His grip was firm on her arms. "I want you there."

"Live with you," Ruth said again, struggling to take it in. "My things . . ."

"Bring your things." Nick shook her in frustration. "What does it matter?"

Ruth shook her head, lifting a hand to push herself away. "You have to give me time to think."

"Damn it, what need is there to think?" He betrayed the depth of his agitation by swearing in English. She was too confused to notice. She might have been prepared for him to ask her to take such a step, but she hadn't been prepared for him to shout it at her.

"I have a need to think," she shot back. "You're asking me to change my life, give up the only home of my own I've ever had."

"I'm asking you to have a home with me." His fingers dug deeper. "I will not go on stealing little moments of time with you."

"You can't, *you* won't! *I* have the final say in my own life. I won't be pressured this way!"

"Pressured? Hell!" Nick stormed to the window, then back to her. "You speak to me of pressures? Five years, *five years* I've waited for you. I wanted a child and must wait until the child grows to a woman." His English began to elude him.

Ruth's eyes grew enormous. "Are you telling me you felt . . . had feelings for me since . . . since the beginning and never told me?"

"What was I to say?" he countered, furiously. "You were seventeen."

"I had a right to make my own choice!" She tossed her hair back and glared at him. "You had no right to make it for me."

"I gave you your choice when the time was right."

"You gave!" she retorted. Indignation nearly chocked her. "You're the director of the company, Davidov, not of my life. How dare you presume to make any decisions for me!"

"My life was also involved," he reminded her. His eyes glittered as he spoke. "Or do you forget?"

"You always treated me like a child," she fumed, ignoring his question. "You never considered that between my childhood and dancing, I was grown up before I ever met you. And now you stand there and tell me you kept something from me for years for my own good. *And* you tell me to pack my things and move in with you without giving it a thought."

"I had no idea such a suggestion would offend you," he said coldly.

"Suggestion?" she repeated. "It came out as an order. I won't be *ordered* to live with you."

"Very well, do as you wish." He gave her a long, steady look. "I have an appointment."

Her eyes opened wider in fresh rage as he moved to the door. "I'm taking some time off," she said impulsively.

Nick paused with his hand on the knob and turned to her. "Rehearsals begin again in seven days," he said, deadly calm. "You will be back or you will be fired. I leave the choice to you."

He walked out without bothering to close the door behind him.

Chapter Fourteen

Lindsay hefted Amanda and settled her into the curve of her hip while Justin skidded a car across the wood-planked floor.

"Dinner in ten minutes, young man," she warned, stepping expertly between the wrecked and parked cars. "Go wash your hands."

"They're not dirty." Justin bowed his blond head over a tiny, flashy racer as if to repair the engine.

Lindsay narrowed her eyes while Amanda squirmed for freedom. "Worth might think otherwise," she said. It was her ultimate weapon.

Justin slipped the toy Ferrari into his pocket and got up. With a weighty, world-weary sigh, he walked from the room.

Lindsay smiled after him. Justin had a healthy respect for the fastidious British butler. She listened to the squeak of her son's tennis shoes as he climbed the stairs. He could have used the downstairs bath, but when Justin Bannion was being a martyr, he liked to do it properly.

It amazed Lindsay, when she had time to think of it, that her son was four years old. He had already outgrown the chunky toddler stage and was lean as a whippet. And, she thought, not without pride, he has his mother's hair and eyes. Glancing around the room, she grimaced at the wreckage of cars and small buildings. And his mother's lack of organization, she mused.

"Not like you at all, is he?" She buried her face in her daughter's neck and earned a giggle.

Amanda was dark, the female image of her father. And like Seth, she was meticulous. Armies of dolls were arranged just so in her room. She showed almost a comical knack for neatly stacking her blocks into buildings. Temper perhaps came from both of her parents, as she wasn't too ladylike to chuck a block at her brother if he infringed on her territory.

With a last kiss, Lindsay set Amanda down and began to gather Justin's abandoned traffic jam. She stopped, car in hand, and shot her daughter a look. "Daddy won't like it if I pick these up."

"Justin's sloppy," Amanda stated with sisterly disdain. At two, she had a penchant for picking up telling phrases.

"No argument there," Lindsay agreed and passed a car from hand to hand. "And he certainly has to learn better, but if Worth walks in here..." She let the thought hang, weighing whose disapproval she would rather face. Worth won. Moving quickly, she began scooping up the evidence. "I'll speak to Justin. We won't have to tell Daddy."

"Tell Daddy what?" Seth demanded from the doorway.

"Uh-oh." Lindsay rolled her eyes to the ceiling, then peered over her shoulder. "I thought you were working."

"I was." He took in the tableau quickly. "Covering up for the little devil again, are you?"

"I sent him to wash his hands." Lindsay pushed the hair out of her eyes and continued to stay on her hands and knees. Amanda walked over to wrap an arm around Seth's leg. Both of them studied her in quiet disapproval. "Oh, please!" She laughed, sitting back on her haunches. "We throw ourselves on the mercy of the court."

"Well." He laid a hand on his daughter's head. "What should the punishment be, Amanda?"

"Can't spank Mama."

"No?" Seth gave Lindsay a wicked grin. Walking over, he pulled her to her feet. "In the interest of justice, I might find it necessary." He gave her a light, teasing kiss.

"Are you open to a bribe?" she murmured.

"Always," he told her as she pressed her mouth more firmly to his.

Justin bounced to the doorway with his freshly scrubbed hands in front of him. He made a face at his parents, then looked down at his sister. "I thought we were going to eat."

An hour later Lindsay rushed down the steps, heading out for her evening ballet class. Spotting another of Justin's cars at the foot of the steps, she picked it up and stuffed it into her bag.

"A life of crime," she muttered and pulled open the front door. "Ruth!" Astonished, she simply stared.

"Hi. Got a room for an escaped dancer and a slightly overweight cat for the weekend?"

"Oh, of course!" She pulled Ruth across the threshold for a huge hug. Nijinsky scrambled from between them, leaped to the floor and stalked away. He wasn't fond of traveling. "It's wonderful to see you. Seth and the children will be so surprised."

Through her first rush of pleasure, Lindsay could feel the hard desperation of Ruth's grip. She drew her away and studied her face. She had no trouble spotting the unhappiness. "Are you all right?"

"Yes." Lindsay's eyes were direct on hers. "No," she admitted. "I need some time."

"All right." She picked up Ruth's bag and closed the door behind them. "Your room's in the same place. Go up and surprise Seth and the children. I'll be back in a couple of hours."

"Thanks."

Lindsay dashed out the door, and Ruth drew a deep breath.

Two days later Ruth sat on the couch, a child on each side of her. She read aloud from one of Justin's books. Nijinsky dozed in a patch of sunlight on the floor. She was feeling more settled.

She should have known that she would find exactly what she had needed at the Cliff House. No questions, no coddling. Lindsay had opened the door, and Ruth had found acceptance and love.

After Ruth had left Nick's office, she'd gone back to her apartment, packed and come directly to Cliffside. She hadn't even thought about it, but had simply followed instinct. Now, after two days, Ruth knew her instincts had been right. There were times when only family could heal.

"I thought you must have bound and gagged them," Seth commented as he strode into the room. "They're not this quiet when they're asleep."

Ruth laughed. Both children went to climb into Seth's lap the moment he sat down.

"They're angels, Uncle Seth." She watched him wrap his arms around both his children. "You should be ashamed of yourself, blackening their names."

"They don't need my help for that." He tugged Amanda's hair. "Worth announced that there was a half-eaten lollipop in someone's bed this morning."

"I was going to finish it tonight," Justin stated, looking earnestly up at his father. "He didn't throw it away, did he?"

"Afraid so."

"Nuts."

"He had a few choice things to say about the state of the sheets," Seth added mildly.

Justin set his mouth—his mother's mouth—into a pout. "Do I have to 'pologize again?"

"I should think so."

"I wanna watch." Amanda was already scrambling down in anticipation.

"I'm always 'pologizing," Justin said wearily. Ruth watched him troop from the room with Amanda trotting to keep up.

"You know, of course," Ruth began, "that Worth adores them."

"Yes, but he'd hate to know his secret was out." Seth could hear both sets of feet clattering down the hall toward the kitchen.

"He always awed me." Ruth set the book aside. "All the months I lived with you I never grew completely used to him."

"No one handles him as well as Lindsay does." Seth sat back and let his mind relax. "He's never yet realized he's being handled."

"There's no one like Lindsay," Ruth said.

"No," Seth said in simple agreement. "No one."

"Was it frightening falling in love with someone so—special?"

He could read the question in her eyes and knew what she was thinking. "Loving's always frightening if it's important. Loving someone special only adds to it. Lindsay scared me to death."

"How strange. I always thought of you as invulnerable and fearless."

"Love makes cowards of all of us, Ruth." The memories of his first months with Lindsay, before their marriage, came back to him. "I nearly lost her once. Nothing's ever frightened me more."

"I've watched you for five years." Ruth was frowning in concentration. "Your love's the same as it was in the very beginning."

"No." Seth shook his head. "I love her more, incredibly more. So I have more to lose."

They both heard her burst through the front door. "God save me from mothers who want Pavlova after five lessons!"

"She's home," Seth said mildly.

"Mrs. Fitzwalter," Lindsay began without preamble as she stormed into the room, "wants her Mitzie to take class with Janet Conner. Never mind that Janet has been taking lessons for two years and Mitzie just started two weeks ago." Lindsay plopped into a chair and glared. "Never mind that Janet has talent and Mitzie has lead feet. Mitzie wants to take class with her best friend, and Mrs. Fitzwalter wants to car pool."

"You, of course, explained diplomatically." Seth lifted a brow.

"I was the epitome of diplomacy. I've been taking Worth lessons." She turned to Ruth. "Mitzie is ten pounds overweight and can't manage first position. Janet's been on toe for two months."

"You might find her another car pool," Ruth suggested.

"I did." Lindsay smiled, pleased with herself. The smile faded as she noted the abnormal quiet. "Where are the children?"

"Apologizing," Seth told her.

"Oh, dear, again?" Lindsay sighed and smiled. Rising, she crossed to Seth. "Hi." She bent and kissed him. "Did you solve your cantilever problem?"

"Just about," he told her and brought her back for a more satisfying kiss.

"You're so clever." She sat on the arm of his chair.

"Naturally."

"And you work too hard. Holed up in that office every day, and on Saturday." She slipped her hand into his. "Let's all go for a walk on the beach."

Seth started to agree, then paused. "You and Ruth go. The kids need a nap. I think I'll join them."

Lindsay looked at him in surprise. The last thing Seth would do on a beautiful Saturday afternoon was take a nap. But his message passed to her quickly, and she turned to Ruth with no change in rhythm. "Yes, let's go. I need some air after Mrs. Fitzwalter."

"All right. Do I need a jacket?"

"A light one."

Lindsay looked back down at Seth as Ruth went to fetch one. "Have I told you today how marvelous you are and how I adore you?"

"Not that I recall." He lifted his hand to her hair. "Tell me now."

"You're marvelous and I adore you." She kissed him again before she rose. "I should warn you that Justin informed me yesterday that he was entirely too old for naps."

"We'll discuss it."

"Diplomatically?" she asked, smiling over her shoulder as she walked from the room.

The air smelled of the sea. Ruth had nearly forgotten how clean and sharp the scent was. The beach was long and rocky, with a noisy surf. An occasional leaf found its way down from the grove on the ridge. One scuttled along the sand in front of them. "I've always loved it here." Lindsay stuck her hands into the deep pockets of her jacket.

"I hated it when we first came," Ruth mused, gazing down the stretch of beach as they walked. "The house, the sound, everything."

"Yes, I know."

Ruth cast her a quick look. Yes, she thought, she would have known. "I don't know when I stopped. It seemed I just woke up one day and found I was home. Uncle Seth was so patient."

"He's a patient man." Lindsay laughed. "At times, infuriatingly so. I rant and rave, and he calmly wins the battle. His control can be frustrating." She studied Ruth's profile. "You're a great deal like him."

"Am I?" Ruth pondered the idea a moment. "I wouldn't have thought myself very controlled lately."

"He has his moments, too." Lindsay reached over to pick up a stone and slipped it into her pockets, a habit she had never broken.

"Lindsay, you've never asked why I came so suddenly or how long I intend to stay."

"It's your home, Ruth. You don't have to explain coming here."

"I told Uncle Seth there was no one else like you."

"Did you?" Lindsay smiled at that and brushed some flying hair from her eyes. "That's the best sort of compliment, I think."

"It's Nick," Ruth said suddenly.

"Yes, I know."

Ruth let out a long breath. "I love him, Lindsay. I'm scared."

"I know the feeling. You've fought, I imagine."

"Yes. Oh, there are so many things." Ruth's voice was suddenly filled with the passion of frustration. "I've tried to work it out in my head these past couple of days, but nothing seems to make sense."

"Being in love never makes sense. That's the first rule." They had come to a clump of rocks, and Lindsay sat.

It was right here, she remembered, that Seth and she had stood that day. She had been in love and frightened because nothing made sense. Ruth had come down from the house with a kitten zipped up in her jacket. She'd been about seventeen and cautious about letting anyone get too close. Maybe she's still being cautious, Lindsay thought, looking back at her. "Do you want to talk about it?"

Ruth hesitated only a moment. "Yes, I think I would."

"Then sit, and start at the beginning."

It was so simple once begun. Ruth told her of the suddenness of their coming together after so many years of working side by side. She told her of the shock of learning he loved her and of the frustrations at having no time together. She left nothing out: the scenes with Leah, Nick's quick mood changes, her own uncertainties.

"Then, the day I left, Nadine spoke to me. She wanted me to know that if Nick and I had a break-up and wouldn't work together, she'd have to let me go. I was furious that we couldn't seem to keep what we had between us between us." She stared out toward the sound, feeling impotent with frustration.

"Before I had a chance to simmer down, Nick was demanding that I give up my apartment and move in with him. Just like that," she added, looking back at Lindsay. "Demanding. He was so infuriating, standing there, shouting at me about what *he* wanted. He tossed in that he'd wanted me for five years and had never said a word. I could hardly believe it. The nerve!"

She paused, dealing with a fresh spurt of anger. "I couldn't stand thinking he'd been directing my life. He was unreasonable and becoming more Russian by the minute. I was to pack up my things and move in with him without a moment's thought. He didn't even ask; he was ordering, as though he were staging his latest ballet. No," she corrected herself and rose, no longer able to sit, "he's more human when he's staging. He didn't once ask me what my feelings were. He just threw this at me straight after my little session with Nadine and after the dreadful week of taping."

Ruth ran out of steam all at once and sat back down. "Lindsay, I've never been so confused in my life."

Idly, Lindsay jiggled the stone in her pocket. She had listened throughout Ruth's speech without a single interruption. "Well," she said finally, "I have a firm policy against offering advice." Pausing, she gazed out at the sea. "And policies are made to be broken. How well do you know Nick?"

"Not as well as you do," Ruth said without thinking. "He was in love with you." The words were out before she realized she had thought them. "Oh, Lindsay."

"Oh, indeed." She faced Ruth directly. "When I first joined the company, Nadine was struggling to keep it going. Nick's coming gave it much-needed momentum, but there were internal problems, financial pressures outsiders are rarely aware of. I know you think Nadine was hard—she undoubtedly was—but the company is everything to her. It's easier for me to understand that now with the distance. I didn't always.

"In any case," she continued, "Nick's coming was the turning point. He was very young, thrown into the spotlight in a strange country. He barely spoke coherent English. French, Italian, a bit of German, but he had to learn English from the ground up. Of all people, you should understand what it's like to be in a strange country with strange customs, to be the outsider."

"Yes," Ruth murmured. "Yes, I do."

"Well, then." Lindsay wrapped her arms around her knee. "Try to picture a twenty-year-old who had just made the most important decision of his life. He had left his country, his friends, his family. Yes, he has a family," Lindsay said, noting Ruth's surprise. "It wasn't easy for him, and the first years made him very careful. There were a lot of people out there who were very eager to exploit him—his story, his background. He learned to edit his life. When I met him, he was already Davidov, a name in capital letters."

She took a moment, watching the surf fly up on the rocks. "Yes, I was attracted to him, very attracted. Maybe half in love for a while. It might have been the same for him. We were dancers and young and ambitious. Maybe if my parents hadn't had the accident, maybe if I had stayed with the company, something would have developed between us. I don't know. I met Seth." Lindsay smiled and glanced back up at the Cliff House. "What I do know is that whatever Nick and I might have had, it wouldn't have been the right choice for either of us. There's no one for me but Seth. Now or ever."

"Lindsay, I didn't mean to pry." Ruth gestured helplessly.

"You're not prying. We're all bound up in this. That's why I'm breaking my policy." She paused another moment. "Nick talked to me in those days because he needed someone. There were few people he felt he could trust. He thought he could trust me. If there are things he hasn't told you, it's simply because it's become a habit of his not to dwell on what he left behind. Nick is a man who looks ahead. But he feels, Ruth; don't imagine he doesn't."

"I know he does," Ruth said quietly. "I've only wanted to share it with him."

"When he's ready, you will." She said it simply. "Nick made ballet first in his life out of choice or necessity, take your pick. From what you've told me, it appears something else is beginning to take the driver's seat. I imagine it scares him to death.''

"Yes." Ruth remembered what her uncle had said to her. "I hadn't thought that he'd feel that way, too."

"When a man, especially a man with a flair for words and staging, asks a woman to live with him so clumsily, I'd guess he was scared right out of his shoes." She smiled a little and touched Ruth's hand. "Now, as for this Leah and the rest of this nonsense about your relationship interfering with your careers or vice versa, you should know better. After five years with the company you should be able to spot basic jealousy when it hits you in the face."

Ruth let out a sigh. "I've always been able to before."

"This time the stakes were higher. Love can cloud the issue." She studied Ruth in silence for a moment. "And how much have you been willing to give him?"

Ruth opened her mouth to speak, then shut it again. "Not enough," she admitted. "I was afraid, too. He's such a strong man, Lindsay; his personality is overwhelming. I didn't want to lose myself." She looked at Lindsay searchingly. "Is that wrong?"

"No. If you were weak and bent under every demand he handed out, he wouldn't be in love with you." She took Ruth's hand and squeezed it. "Nick needs a partner, Ruth, not a fan."

"He can be so arrogant. So impossible."

"Yes, bless him."

Ruth laughed and hugged her. "Lindsay, I needed to come home."

"You've come." Lindsay returned the hug. "Do you love him?"

"Yes. Yes, I love him."

"Then go pack and go after him. Time's too precious. He's in California." She smiled at Ruth's puzzled face. "I called Nadine this morning. I'd already decided to break my policy."

Chapter Fifteen

Nick's feet pounded into the sand. He was on his third mile. The sun was rising slowly, casting rose-gold glints into the ocean. Dawn had been pale and gray when he had started. He had the beach to himself. It was too early for even the most enthusiastic jogger. He liked the lonely stretch of sand turning gold under the sun, the empty cry of gulls over his head and the whooshing sound of the waves beside him.

The only pressures here were the ones he put on his own body. Like dancing, running could be a solitary challenge. And here, too, he could put his mind above the pain. Today, if he ran hard enough, far enough, he might stop thinking of Ruth.

How could he have been so stupid? Nick cursed himself again and increased his pace. *What timing! What style!* He had meant to give her more space, meant to wait until the scene was right. Nothing had come out the way he had intended. Had he actually ordered her to pack? What had possessed him? Anger, frustration, need. Fear. The choreography he had so carefully devised had become stumbling missteps.

He had wanted to ease her into living with him, letting her grow used to the first commitment before he slid her into marriage. He had destroyed it all with temper and arrogance.

Once he had begun, he had been unable to stop himself. And how she had looked at him! First stunned, then furious. How could he have been so clumsy? There had been countless women in his life, and he had never had such trouble telling them what he felt—what he didn't feel. How many languages could he make love in? Why, when it finally mattered, had he struck out like a blundering fool? Yet it had been so with every step in his courtship of Ruth.

Courtship! He berated himself and kept running as the sun grew higher. He set himself a punishing rhythm. What courtship had he given her? He had taken her like a crazed man the first time, and when he had told her he loved her, had there been any finesse? A schoolboy would have shown more care!

Well out at sea a school of dolphins took turns leaping into the air; a beautifully choreographed water ballet. Nick kept running.

She won't be back, he thought grimly. Then in despair—good God, what will I do? Will I bury myself in the company and have nothing else, like poor Nadine? Is this what all the years have been for? Every time I dance, she'll be there, just out of reach. She'll go to another company, dance with Mitchell or Kirminov. The thought made his blood boil.

I'll drag her back. He pounded on, letting the pain fill him. She's so young! What right do I have to force her back to me? Could I? It isn't right; a man doesn't drag a woman back when she leaves him. There's the pride. I won't.

The hell I won't, he thought suddenly and turned back toward the house. He never slackened his pace. *The hell I won't.*

Ruth pulled up in front of the house and sat in the rented car, letting the engine idle. The house was two stories of wind- and salt-weathered cedar and gleaming glass. Very impressive, Uncle Seth, she decided, admiring the clean, sharp lines and lavish use of open space he had used in designing this house.

Swallowing, she wondered for the hundredth time how to approach the situation. All the neat little speeches she had rehearsed on the plane seemed hopelessly silly or strained.

"Nick, I thought we should talk," she tried out loud, then laid her forehead on the steering wheel. Brilliant. Why don't I just use: "Hello, Nick, I was just passing by, thought I'd drop in?" That's original.

Just do it, she told herself. Just go up there and knock on the door and let it happen. Moving quickly, Ruth shut off the engine and slid out of the car. The six steps leading to the front door looked impossibly high. Taking a deep breath, as she had so many other times for a *jeté* from the wings, she climbed them.

Now knock, she ordered herself as she stared at the door. Just lift your hand, close it into a fist and knock. It took her a full minute to manage it. She waited, the breath backing up in her lungs. No answer. With more determination she knocked again. And waited.

Unable to bear the suspense any longer, Ruth put her hand on the knob and turned. She almost leaped back when it opened to her touch. The locks and bolts of Manhattan were more familiar.

The living room apparently took up the entire first floor. The back wall was almost completely in glass, featuring a stunning panorama of the Pacific. For a moment Ruth forgot her anxiety. She had seen other buildings of her uncle's design, but this was a masterpiece.

The floor was wood, graced by a few very plain buff-colored rugs. He had placed no paintings on the walls. The ocean was art enough. Trinkets were few, but she lifted an exquisite old brass silent butler that pleased her tremendously. There was a bar with shelves behind it lined with glasses of varying colors and shapes. The sofa was thick and deep and piled with pillows. A gleaming mahogany grand piano stood in the back of the room, its top opened wide. Ruth went to it and lifted a sheet of staff paper.

Musical notes dotted it, with Nick's meticulous handwriting in the margins. The Russian writing was unintelligible to her, but she began to pick out the melody on the piano.

His new ballet? She listened carefully to the unfamiliar music. With a smile she set the paper back in place. He was amazing, she decided. Davidov had the greatest capacity for work of anyone she had ever known.

But where was he?

Ruth turned to look around the room again. Could he have gone back to New York? Not with the door unlocked and pages of his new ballet still on the piano! She glanced at her watch and suddenly remembered: She was still on east coast time. Oh, for heaven's sake, she thought as she quickly calculated the time difference. It was early! He was probably still in bed.

Slowly, Ruth walked to the stairs and peered up. I can't just go up there. She pressed her lips together. I could call. She opened her mouth and shut it again on a sound of annoyance. What could she say? *Yoo-hoo, Nick, time to get up?* She lifted her fingers to her lips to stifle a nervous giggle.

Taking a deep breath, Ruth put her hand on the banister and started to climb.

Nick opened the double glass doors that led from the back deck to the living room. He was breathing hard. His sweat shirt was dampened in a long vee from neck to hem. The exertion had helped. He felt cleaner, clearer. He would go up and have a shower and then work through the day on the new ballet. His plans to go east and drag Ruth back with him were the thoughts of a crazy man.

Halfway into the room, he stopped. The scent of wildflowers overwhelmed him. God! Would he never escape her?

What right had she to do this to him, to haunt him wherever he went? Damn her, he thought furiously. I've had enough of this!

Striding to the phone, he lifted it and punched out Ruth's number in New York. Without any idea of what he would say, Nick waited in blind fury for her to answer. With another curse, he hung up again. Where the devil is she? The company? No, he shook his head immediately. *Lindsay.* Of course, where else would she go?

Nick picked up the phone again and had pushed four numbers when a sound caught his attention. Frowning, he glanced toward the stairs. Ruth walked down, her own face creased in a frown.

Their eyes met immediately.

"So, there you are," she said and hoped the words didn't sound as foolish as they felt. "I was looking for you."

With infinite care Nick replaced the phone receiver in its cradle. "Yes?"

Though his response was far from gracious, Ruth came down the rest of the steps. "Yes. Your door was unlocked. I hope you don't mind that I just came in."

"No."

She fidgeted nervously, concentrating all her effort into a smile. "I noticed you've started work on your new ballet."

"I've begun, yes." The words were carefully spaced. His eyes never left hers.

Unable to bear the contact, Ruth turned to wander the room. "This is a lovely place. I can see why you come whenever you have the chance. I've always loved the ocean. We stayed in a house on the Pacific once in Japan." She began to ramble on, hardly knowing what she said but needing to fill the space with words. Nick remained silent, studying her back as she stared out to sea.

Realizing his muscles were balled tight, Nick forced them to relax. He hadn't heard a word she had said.

"Do you come to enjoy the view?" he demanded, interrupting her.

Ruth winced, then composed her face before she turned. "I came to see you," she told him. "I have things to say."

"Very well." He gestured with his hand. "Say them."

His unconscious gesture stiffened her spine. "Oh, I intend to. Sit down."

His brow lifted at the order. After a moment he moved to the sofa. "I'm sitting."

"Do you practice being insufferable, Davidov, or is it a natural talent?"

Nick waited a moment, then leaned back against the pillows. "You've traveled three thousand miles to tell me this?"

"And more," Ruth shot back. "I've no intention of being buried by you, professionally or personally. We'll speak of the dancing first."

"By all means." Nick lifted his hands and let them fall. "Please continue."

"I'm a good dancer, and whether you partner me or not, I'll continue to be a good dancer. In the company you can tell me to dance until my feet drop off, and I'll do it. You're the director."

"I'm aware of that."

Ruth glared at him. "But that's where it stops. You don't direct my life. Whatever I do or don't do is my choice and my responsibility. If I choose to take a dozen lovers or live like a hermit, you have nothing whatever to say about it."

"You think not?" His words were cool enough, his position still easy against the pillows, but fury had leaped into his eyes.

"I *know* you." Ruth took another step toward him. "As long as I'm free, until I make a personal commitment, no one has any business interfering with how I live, with what I do. No one questions you, Davidov. You wouldn't permit it. Well, neither will I." She put her hands on her hips. "If you think I'll run along like a good little girl and pack my bags because you tell me to, you're sadly mistaken. I'm not a little girl, and I won't be told what to do. I make my own choices." She walked toward him.

"You always expect everyone to cheerfully do your bidding," she continued, still fuming. "But you'd better prepare yourself for a shock. I've no intention of being your underling. Partners, Davidov, in every sense. And I won't live with you; it's not good enough. If you want me, you'll have to marry me. That's it." Ruth crossed her arms over her chest and waited.

Nick straightened slowly, then, taking another moment, rose. "Is that an ultimatum?"

"You bet it is."

"I see." He studied her consideringly. "It seems you give me no choice. You will wish to be married in New York?"

Ruth opened her mouth, and when there were no words, cleared her throat. "Well, yes—I suppose."

"Did you have in mind a small ceremony or something large?"

With the impetus gone, she stared at him in confusion. "I don't know...I hadn't thought..."

"Well, you can decide on the plane, yes?" He gave her an odd smile. "Shall I make reservations for a flight now?"

"Yes. No," she said when he turned for the phone. Nick tilted his head and waited. "All right, yes, go ahead." Ruth went to the windows again and stared out. Why, she asked herself, does it seem so wrong?

"Ruth." He waited until she faced him again. "I've told you I love you, I've said the same words to women I don't even remember. Words mean little."

She swallowed and felt the ache begin. The whole expanse of the room separated them.

"I have not shown you, as I wanted to, the way I felt. You make me clumsy." He spread his fingers. "A difficult thing for a dancer to admit. If I were not clumsy, I could tell you that my life is not my life without you. I could tell you that you are the heart of it, the muscle, the bone. I could tell you there is only emptiness and aching without you. I could tell you that to be your partner, your husband, your lover, is what I want more than breath. But..." He shook his head. "You make me clumsy, and I can only tell you that I love you and hope it is enough."

"Nick!" She ran for him, and he caught her before she was halfway across the room.

He held her tightly, just filling himself with the joy of having her in his arms again. "When I saw you walk down the stairs, I thought it was a dream. I thought I had gone mad."

"I thought you'd still be asleep."

"Sleep? I don't think there has been sleep since you left me." He drew her away. "Never again," he said fiercely. "Hate me, shout at me, but don't leave me again." His mouth came down on hers and smothered her promise.

Her answer was as wild and heated as his demand. She tangled her fingers into his hair, pressing him closer, wanting to drown in the current that raged between them. Need soared through her, a raw, urgent hunger that made her mouth grow more desperate under his. Desire came in an avalanche of sensations; his taste, his scent, the thick soft texture of his hair in her hands.

"I love you." Her mouth formed the words but made no sound. "I love you."

She felt him release the zipper at her back and let the dress slip to the floor. Nick let out a low groaning murmur as he stroked his hands down her sides.

"So small, *lyubovnitsa,* I fear always to hurt you."

"I'm a dancer," she reminded him, thrilling to the touch of his hands over the thin silk of her chemise. "Strong as an ox." They lowered to the sofa and lay tangled together. "I was afraid," she murmured, closing her eyes as his hands gently aroused her. "Afraid to trust you, afraid to love you, afraid to lose you."

"Both of us." He pulled her close and just held her. "No more."

Ruth slipped her hand under his shirt to lay it on his heart. *Davidov,* she thought. How many years had she worshipped the legend? Now the man was hers. And she his. She held his heart and was sure of it. Smiling, she pressed her lips to his neck and lingered there.

"Davidov?"

"Mmm?"

"Are you really going to accept that ultimatum?"

His hand reached for her breast. "I've thought about it. It seems for the best. You were very fierce. I think I'll humor you."

"Oh, do you?" Her smile was in her voice.

"Yes, but I will not permit your dozen lovers unless they are all me." He took his mouth on a teasing journey along her jaw line. "I think I should keep you busy enough."

"Maybe," she said and sighed luxuriously as he began to unlace the front of her chemise.

His mouth came to hers and swept her away even as he continued to undress her. "I will be a very jealous husband. Unreasonable, perhaps violent.'' He lifted his face to smile down at her. "Very hard to live with. Do I still call for the plane?''

Ruth opened her eyes and looked into his. She smiled. "Yes. Tomorrow.''

*   *   *   *   *

Summer romance has never been so hot!

SILHOUETTE

SUMMER Sizzlers

A collection of hot summer reading by three of
Silhouette's hottest authors:

Ann Major
Paula Detmer Riggs
Linda Lael Miller

Put some sizzle into your summer reading. You
won't want to miss your ticket to summer fun—with
the best summer reading under the sun!

You, too, can write in the
LANGUAGE OF LOVE with Silhouette's

FREE
ELEGANT STATIONERY

An elegant box of stationery—perfect for yourself or to give as a gift! Each sheet is beautifully imprinted with specially commissioned artwork from the Nora Roberts Language of Love Collection. Every box includes 24 sheets, six each of four different designs, all in full color, plus 24 matching envelopes.

This stationery will not be sold in retail stores. See proof-of-purchase on next page for details. (Retail value of stationery: $12.95)

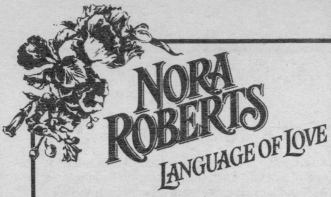

NORA ROBERTS

LANGUAGE OF LOVE

FREE Floral Stationery

Just mail us four proofs-of-purchase from any of the
NORA ROBERTS Language of Love titles 1 to 12, plus
$2.75 for postage and handling (check or money
order—please do not send cash) payable to Silhouette
Reader Service to:

In the U.S.
Language of Love Stationery
Silhouette Books
3010 Walden Ave.
P.O. Box 1396
Buffalo, NY 14269-1396

In Canada
Language of Love Stationery
Silhouette Books
P.O. Box 609
Fort Erie, Ontario
L2A 5X3

(Offer expires September 30, 1992)

Please allow six weeks for delivery.

ORDER FORM

Name _____

Address _____ Apt. _____

City _____ State/Prov _____

Daytime Phone # _____ Zip/Postal Code _____

Silhouette ®

LOLPOP-R

LANGUAGE OF LOVE
PROOF-OF-
PURCHASE